BEFORE THE FALL

And

OTHER SHORT STORIES

Volume 4

Send inquiries to:

Digital Legend Publishing
1994 Forest Bend Dr.
Cottonwood Heights, UT 84121

Visit www.Digitalegend.com/Carol

or write to info@digitalegend.com
or call toll free: 877-222-1960

Printed in the United States of America

ISBN:978-1-937735-36-4

Interior and cover design by Alisha Bishop

Before the Fall

And

Other Short Stories

Volume 4

Christmas Carol Kauffman

Compiled by Marcia Kauffman Clark

DIGITAL
LEGEND

New York

Table of Contents

Foreword

Nelson E. Kauffman preached in special services at the Maple Grove Mennonite Church near Belleville, PA in the fall of 1953. He mentioned to the local pastor that he was looking for a young man to assist in the ministry of his congregation in Hannibal, MO. I had graduated from Belleville high school that year and was looking for a place to fulfill an obligation to alternative service as a 1-w worker. In March I moved into the mission home with the Kauffman family and began two years as an orderly at Levering Hospital.

At that time there were two female voluntary service workers, Ruth King, who wrote the Forward for Volume 2, Fern Stutzman, and one young man, Mel Lapp, who wrote the Forward for Volume 3. We all enjoyed living at the mission home. I shared a room with Mel. The Kauffman family in the large house consisted of Nelson and Carol and their children, James and Marcia in school and Stanlee, when home during his summer break from Hesston College.

We four service workers assisted Nelson and the congregation in its witness in the local community. There were the regular services of the church, revival meetings, street meetings downtown, services at rest homes, and a radio broadcast , "Christ For Today", that Nelson provided weekly Sunday morning sermons on the local station. There was plenty of work for all in the three-story house with eight residents plus continual visitors; many unexpected. Hannibal was a full day drive between Goshen Mennonite College in Goshen, Indiana and Hesston Mennonite College in Hesston Kansas a perfect place to stop and visit the Kauffmans.

The atmosphere in the mission home is reflected in the forms of address. We did not address Nelson and Carol by name. It was always Brother Kauffman and Sister Kauffman. The terms, brother and sister, were not required or demanded. They just seemed to fit and express the respect and affection we experienced and felt.

I don't think that I had read any of Sister Kauffman's stories or books before coming to Hannibal. I do remember that she spent time alone writing in her room off the kitchen. Carol was a small strong woman. She was principled and kind. Reading her works after learning to know her in person was a special blessing for me.

Nelson traveled a lot in church-wide circles in the interests of missions, revival, and education. Mel and I would often take him to and from the train at Palmyra or Quincy. Carol put up with the pranks of young folks around the mission home with grace and humor. The usual response from her was, "Oh dear!" I suppose that is where Marcia learned it.

The weekly radio program was expensive. Brother Kauffman and our quartet visited Mennonite churches in southeast Iowa in fund raising. Brother K would preach and we would sing. I made some friends in these Iowa churches and eventually married a young woman from the Sugar Creek church at Wayland. Nelson gave the sermon at our wedding.

My life was broadened and enriched by the two years with the Kauffman's at Hannibal. Nelson and Carol were excellent mentors moving me toward a lifetime in pastoral ministry. Carol's commitment to Christ and His people lives on in the memories of those who knew her personally as well as in the thousands of pages of her published works. It is wonderful that we have the privilege of reading Carol's short stories that she started writing when a student at Hesston College in Hesston, Kansas. Her talent to write is unending as was her unwavering testimony that she shared, through her gifted pen that continues to be available to us today in this fourth volume, forty-four years after her untimely death. Thank you Sister Kauffman for your personal talent, given to each of us as we unite our love for our Lord and Savior, on who's birthday we celebrate in which you were born.

—Robert L. Hartzler

Preface

Once again, I have the wonderful privilege of sharing more short stories with all of you in Volume IV. This volume has several more of Mothers powerfully created stories that you have not been able to read for seventy-four years; unless you went to the Historical Library in Goshen, Indiana and searched page by page to find them. What a wonderful privilege for me to do that for each one of you.

What a tremendous blessing that we live in a day and age that we can scan and photo-copy pages from the original Youth's Christian Companion's. How fortunate we are that the publishers were inspired years ago to keep these priceless original copies in the large bound volumes for us to read in 2012.

Mother would be one hundred eleven years old this coming Christmas morning. She was only thirty-six years old when she wrote the first story in this volume; four years before I was born. Each one is different than all the others, with a very special message to share with all readers yearning to have more. In each one of her "made up" stories, she always shared her undeniable faith in our Heavenly Father. She knew He loves, guides and directs each one of us; that He has concerns for our individual lives, full of varied experiences, and that He knows our thoughts and desires to bless us as we continually seek His guidance. She knew how to write tender, heart felt stories because of personal experiences she had or had seen in others, even at the tender age of 36.

It is my desire this day, and I also know for sure that it would be Mother's, if she were writing this Preface, that we rededicate our lives in service to others; that we continue to be examples of righteousness and goodness, like she continually wrote about. My heart is full of gratitude again to have the privilege to share these priceless "gems" because that is exactly what they are.

My gratitude is unending to my publisher Boyd J. Tuttle and his daughter Alisha, for helping me bring this fourth volume to you. Thank you, Victoria Waters, from the Historical Library in Goshen, Indiana. Your most valued assistance in providing the extra photo-copied pages I needed for two stories in this volume was a great blessing.

Each of the previous volumes have the blessing of fond memories of "workers" who spent time with our family at the Hannibal Mennonite Mission Church and parsonage. Robert Hartzler lived with our family when I was twelve years old. Thank you Bob, for sharing your memories with us. And lastly, thank you Mother for your gifted, endlessly creative right-handed pencil, but most of all, thank you again for the privilege of calling you Mother.

Before The Fall

By Christmas Carol Kauffman, age 36, Hannibal, Missouri
Originally published March 15, 22 and 29, 1939
in the Youth's Christian Companion

Sue sat on her trunk by the window and swung her right leg back and forth. She bit her lips and rolled her handkerchief into a tight wad. Ella was humming softly an original chorus which was one of her favorite pastimes. It made Sue nervous. The wad in her hand got tighter and smaller, and her leg went faster.

"What's that you're humming?" She said irritably to her sister who was tying her apron around her waist.

"Oh, I don't know," she smiled; "just humming."

"Well, I wish you'd stop it. It's a silly habit you've got."

"O.K," sighed Ella. She was used to being told such things by her sister who was older than she.

"How did you get along with your class this morning?" Sue's voice was harsh.

"Why—shy—all right, I think, Sue. Why? Did you hear that I didn't?"

"No; but I just wondered. You haven't had much experience in teaching, and I didn't notice that you studied your lesson enough to handle that class. Did they talk?"

"Yes," Sue looked out the window drearily.

"Didn't you think they would?"

"Well, I didn't know if they would for you or not. I know they would for me, because I know how to ask questions to make them talk. I thought Brother B— was going to ask me to take it. I had it the last time he was sick, and the girls said that they wished I was their regular teacher." Sue eyed her sister curiously and waited for some comment, but Ella made none.

"Did the girls say anything about me this morning?"

"Not that I heard."

"Didn't Mary?"

"Not that I heard, Sue."

"Huh. Mary told me she'd never stay for class if they had anyone else take it when Marie was gone. That's just it. You don't know who to believe anymore. How did they treat you, anyway?"

"Just all right." Ella said, "Joe's family is coming down for dinner,"

"They are?" Sue spoke in disgust, "Oh, dear. Who asked them then, to come?"

"Well, Mother did. You know they moved yesterday and are partly torn up, yet, and why not? We have plenty of everything fixed."

"Well, I know—but—"

Sue sat at the window and thought things over and then went downstairs to help.

"Ella isn't even attractive," thought Sue as she looked out over the orchard; and sometime uses poor English, and she certainly doesn't have "it" at all. She was just cut out to be an old maid—but I wasn't. And Sue got abruptly to her feet and stood before the mirror admiring her hair, her eyes, her lips and her form. She winked at the lovely girl she saw in the mirror and gave her head a toss.

"You're going to make a mark in the world some day", she said proudly, and shook a finger at herself, "Yet young lady, you weren't given all these talents just to bury them. Now hold your head up and stop that frowning for you know perfectly well that neither your sister, nor any other girl can ever put you in the shade in teaching a Sunday school class, or singing or speaking, or anything else for that matter; for there are not many girls in the world like Sue Smith, and you know it!" And the girl in the mirror got another confident wink. She took out a clean handkerchief from the drawer and put a dab of perfume on her eyebrows, and pinned on her blue organdy apron. It was really way to pretty to wear.

Ella talked pleasantly to Joe Flangenweiler, and shook hands with all the children and hurried to the kitchen, where Joe's wife was busy slicing potatoes.

"Say, Ella," and the visiting lady smiled kindly. "Darlene says you make a real good Sunday school teacher."

Just then Sue entered the kitchen. She smiled and spoke to Mrs. Flangenweiler without really looking at her. She was busy finding another paring knife. Ella hurried to the cellar for some pickles and back in no time.

"Did you hear what I said a while ago, Ella?"

"Darlene says you make a really good Sunday school teacher."

Ella blushed a little. "Oh—I'm—I hope I will, maybe, someday. I enjoy it for some reason, but I haven't had much experience."

"Well, I think the best teachers are those who feel they must always do better next time."

"That's right." Spoke Ella's mother thoughtfully.

"But more than that," added Mrs. Flangenweiler, "the children really like a teacher who they believe lives the things they teach to others. They can tell the difference too," concluded the other. Sue coughed and said nothing. She wished dinner was over so she could go upstairs to be alone. Ella and the two women talked about the various happenings in the church and the neighborhood and had a pleasant time preparing the meal. Sue said so little that at length Mrs. Flangenweiler ventured to ask, "Are you not feeling well, today, Sue?"

She shrugged her shoulders and said, "Why?"

"You are so quiet, I always thought that you were a big talker," laughed Mrs. Flangenweiler, teasingly. She shrugged her shoulders and looked up in surprise. "I do have a headache and am going up to take a nap after dinner."

"Are you still working at the Browns?"

"No, I quit there last night." Mrs. Flangenweiler looked up again.

"You did? Did you know that Mrs. Birdell wants a girl? Maybe you can get that place." She laughed mockingly.

"No thanks," I don't want it; I know Mrs. Birdell too well."

She laughed mockingly again. "I'm going to town next week."

Those sighs! How she hated them. They were provoking and uncalled for. Why couldn't her mother act young and jolly like Edith's mother? She was jolly with her girls and took their part, and they were popular too; never without a boyfriend! Now that was another thing she could not understand. Why, oh why, didn't she have a real boyfriend? It was not because she wasn't pretty and cute, and it absolutely wasn't because she wasn't smart; and she could do anything any other girl could do. It must—it must be because her mother was so strict and old-fashioned, and because Ella was too much like her mother. She would break away from them. She was born to be different, and she would be too. The rest of the family traits from both sides of the house were wonderfully blended in Sue Smith and she knew it.

Immediately after dinner Sue excused herself abruptly.

"Mother, you have plenty of help here. I want to take a nap."

"Of course", spoke Mrs. Flangenweiler, "you just run along. We can get the dishes done."

"I thought so." Sue left the room. At the downstairs door she hesitated. Theodore, her brother was in the living room with the men.

"Come here a minute, Theodore. Listen!" She whispered and caught hold of his coat lapel. "Are you having a date tonight with Marietta?"

"Why do you want to know?"

"Are you?" She was very insistent and looked straight into his eyes. "Well, are you?"

"Tell me why you want to know." Theodore drew back.

"Well, you are. I know it. And who's going along?"

"Nobody."

"What's Marvin going to do tonight?"

"What in the world are you up to, Sue?" Theodore frowned and he drew back.

"Well, I'm going to have a date too, and you are going to help me out!"

"Indeed!" Stated Theodore emphatically. Sue's hand on his lapel tightened and her eyes snapped. "Listen; Marvin is a dandy chap."

"I know that!"

"And he likes me too."

"How do you know that?"

"I just know, I can tell."

"How?" He demanded. "Did he ever tell you?"

"Not in so many words, but I can tell he does. There is more than one way to tell. He always looks at me. A lot too!"

Theodore laughed. "Maybe he can't help it because you—"

"I know he is interested in me. I KNOW!" She hid her face in her brother's shoulder.

"Has he ever asked you for a date?"

"No, that's the trouble. I want you to help me out. He wants to; I know, but—"

"But what?" Theodore was impatient now.

"He's too bashful, and you can help him out!"

"Help him out! Nothin!! Marvin Long isn't as bashful as you suppose. He is as old as I and if he wants a date he will do his own asking."

"But Theodore!" Sue's countenance fell. "I'm tired of being left behind; and if you really love me, you'd take Marvin and me along tonight, and stop being so selfish!"

"Selfish?"

"Yes! You and Marietta never ask anyone to go along."

"Well, listen here, Sister Sue," and Theodore put a strong hand on both of Sue's shoulders. "I'm surprised. Would you actually enjoy yourself with Marvin if I had to suggest it to him?"

"Well, I don't see why not. Other girls' brothers help them out and—"

"Well, that might all be, Sue, although none of my chums do it to my knowledge; but that's one thing I'll never do. I'd hate to think that Marietta's brother was persuaded to do such a thing. If you keep your place and wait on the Lord, you will be happy; but if not, you'll disgrace yourself and all the family."

"Theodore! How can you say such a thing?"

"I mean it. Look at Sadie, for instance."

"Yes, but Marvin is a real Christian."

"Maybe so, and all the more reason why—"

The phone rang. Sue answered.

"Yes, yes. No; this is Sue. Who? Just a minute. Ella!" She cried out impatiently.

"Yes, I thought you went upstairs, Sue."

"Well, I just didn't get up there yet."

Instead of going upstairs, Sue stood close to the phone. Her face turned white, and then red, her hands trembled.

***

"Oh—Oh! Sue caught her breath. "What now? She demanded. "Was that Marvin?"

"Yes, he's coming after me at four o'clock, and—"

"What?"

"Well, now Sue," laughed Ella, "please don't get excited; he's going to take me over to his place to practice."

"Practice what?"

"A quartet."

"Why?"

"For tonight, I suppose."

"And who else is in it?"

"He didn't say."

"Of, all things!" Sue's head did ache now for sure. She sat on the trunk by the window and looked out over the orchard for a long, long time. She was still sitting there when Ella entered humming very softly. She did not turn her head. She could hear her own heart thump.

"Why don't you lie down?"

"I will when I get ready. You think—" For some reason she did not finish her sentence. The hateful words were checked and her eyes dropped. She remembered when a few years ago, Ella lay at the point of death, and several doctors said there was no hope for her recovery. Then Father and Mother called the family together once more, and they fasted and prayed for two days. Father and Mother, Theodore, and Sue all fasted and confessed their faults one to another and prayed and pleaded with God to save Ella's life, only for His glory. How earnestly Sue had prayed and talked on and on with the Lord about her only sister, held her hand, and kissed it tenderly, stayed by her side, and watched every move she made, while the others took their rest. As Ella stood there now, some sweet expression on her face that, Sue had seen before made her words fail her. When had she first allowed this spirit to enter her heart? It troubled Sue a little. She tried to sleep, but could not.

She was called upon to lead the singing in church that night. She held her head up and sang with all her might. Surely there was no other girl in the whole church who could do any better. Several times Sue found Marvin looking at her. She smiled. But when the quartet sang, Sue could not smile, hard as she thought and tried. "Ella didn't do too badly," she admitted to herself, "but, I could have done a lot better."

Marvin brought Ella home after church. Sue asked Ella not one question but immediately went to bed.

The next morning Sue persuaded Theodore to take her to town.

"Why do you not want to take me, Theodore?" She asked after they had gone about a mile.

"Well, it would be alright, Sue, if you—"

"What?" She interrupted impatiently.

"Well, if you would only let the Lord lead you."

"Well, I do."

"In everything, Sue?" She fumbled at her purse.

"Yes," she answered at last.

A light snow was falling, and Sue drew her fur collar closer around her face. By the time they reached town, the snow was falling fast. Sue bought an evening paper and scanned the want ads.

Theodore took her to seven different homes to answer advertisements, but at each place, the mistress had already employed a girl or Sue didn't have sufficient experience in one thing or another.

"You're not supposed to find work in town," declared Theodore. "Lets go back home."

"No!" I'm not going back. I'll go over to Matthews' and try this afternoon. I'll not give up yet."

"But Sue, they are not of our faith; for certain they are far from it,"

"What if they are? They are nice people. Mrs. Matthews will help me, I know. Take me over there."

"What will Mother say?"

"She won't say—well, what if she does? She has something to say about everything, anyway."

They stopped at a small restaurant for dinner and while Theodore was taking off his coat. Sue went over to the man at a desk in the corner. Theodore looked up in astonishment. The man was smiling at Sue and was talking to her in low tones. He scanned her from head to foot. "Tomorrow at seven." Theodore heard him say, and Sue wrote something on a piece of paper he handed to her.

"You're not going to work here." Sue sat down opposite her brother and smiled at the man at the desk.

"Why not?" She retorted.

"This is no place for a Christian girl to work."

"Why not? If I can get some experience waiting on tables here, I can get a job in one of these fine homes."

"The folks will have a spell."

"Then, they will have to have a spell. I'm twenty-two, already; and I've got to earn something."

Theodore left his sister at the Matthews' home and drove home with a heavy heart. Saturday night Theodore stopped at the restaurant. Sue was dressed in a stiffly starched uniform, and was busy when he entered, so he waited near the door.

"Good evening," spoke the manager.

"Good evening."

"Your sister is a peach."

Theodore did not answer. He did not like the man's eyes, nor the way he watched Sue as she hurried back and forth, gracefully carrying glasses and trays, smiling always, and glancing at herself in the large mirrors.

"Won't you take a seat?"

"No, I came to take Sue home."

"Home?"

"Yes, for Sunday."

The man laughed. "Sunday! People are here on Sunday as well as on Saturday. Our best business is on Sunday."

"But didn't my sister say she wanted Sunday off?"

"No, I can't let her off." The man rapped his hand on the glass counter. Theodore looked troubled. Sue came over at length.

"I came for you." Sue looked at the manager. They exchanged smiles.

"Can I?" she asked sweetly.

"I need you Susie Girl. Look here. You're the best girl I've ever hired, and I'm going to keep you. See? She can't go."What will the folks say if you work on Sunday?"

"I can't help it. I'll lose my job if I get off. I'll talk to him all week and see if I can't persuade him to let me off every other Sunday; see?"

"Where do you stay?"

"I have a room at the Matthews'."

"What time do you get off?"

"Well, I get off every afternoon for two hours, and at night it varies some."

"And do you walk way over to the Matthews alone after dark?"

"Oh, not always. Mr. Webb lives down the way and takes me along."

"Oh, Sue!"

"What's the matter, Theodore? You act like I'm a four year old. He's awfully nice to me and he respects me, too."

"I suppose."

Theodore looked at his sister a long time. She tried to evade his eyes. She must go. She dare not neglect her work to stand and talk to him. Mr. Webb was looking impatient. She hurried away, and Theodore left. Once outside he looked back. He saw the manager wink at Sue.

The next Saturday Theodore called again. This time Sue got ready and went along home without a word. They were halfway home, and very little had been spoken by either of them.

"So Mr. Webb let you off every other Sunday to keep peace with the family?"

"Well, that's the way he put it. He does not understand, Theodore."

"But—but you do Sue. Surely you understand that in order to keep your Christian stand and experience, you must attend church whenever possible, and—"

"I do."

"When people ask about you, we hate to tell them that you work in a restaurant on Sunday!"

"Oh, well, I'm taking care of myself all right."

"Are you sure?" This made Sue half angry.

"I know a lot of church-goers who sit around on Sunday afternoon and talk about their crops and things, and in God's sight, they might as well be working."

"Mr. Webb says I can sing well enough to sing in a broadcast some day."

Theodore made no answer. Sue waited for one a little longer.

"If Ella can sing good enough for the church, and I can't, then maybe I can sing for someone else. I've got talent, and I can sing and I am not going to bury it."

"Have you consecrated it to the Lord?"

"Certainly! But the Lord isn't the church."

"Did Marvin take Ella home last Sunday night?"

"Yes."

"Well, that's another thing that seems queer to me. Why did he pick on her when I'm nearer to his age? I've sat at home and tried to be good all these years and—"

"Years?"

"Yes—years, while other girls went out and had a good time, but since I'm in town. I can have lots of attention without half—I mean have nice boys pay attention to me."

"You startle me! You are changing fast."

"No, I'm not! You're just finding it out. Maybe that's so. I wish you'd quit that place."

"Why?" Nice people come in there to eat, Doctors, lawyers, and business men."

"With other men's wives, I suppose?"

"Well, sometimes. Mr. Webb told me since I am there his business has picked up and I get really good tips quite often too."

"I see, you got a new coat already."

"Isn't it pretty? I got some other things I've been wanting for a long time, and things that I couldn't get before."

"The next time I bring Mother to town, I'll bring her here to eat." Sue sat up erect. She caught her breath. Dread seized her. Something was wrong. He looked Sue right in the face."

"OK?"

Sue was strangely bewildered, and she scarcely understood why. Never before had she been ashamed of her own Mother. She would not admit that she was ashamed of her now. It wasn't that. But her mother would look so peculiar sitting in a place like this, so utterly incongruous, she would not enjoy the foods prepared and served as they do at such a place—and—she would be too busy to pay much attention to her, and that might hurt her feelings —oh, such a mixture of flimsy excuses pressed upon her one after another, until she almost felt like crying. She shuddered and did feel like crying this time. It is impossible to tell why if she had to. They were at the gate now, and Sue had not answered.

It is impossible for a girl to be slipping and yet hide from her parents. It is possible for a girl to be slipping and hide it from her Pastor. And sometimes a girl actually succeeds in hiding it from herself. An exalted opinion and one's ability to reason and argue and be most sincere, that deceives the sincere with what God calls right and honest with faith in one's ambitions, and intense longings to get ahead of others, can blind one from doing what's right.

She put forth an effort to act nice when she went home. She helped her mother and talked kindly to Ella most of the time. If they tried to accuse her of being proud since she went to town, she would show them she wasn't. Sue noticed that Mother's step lagged a little and she asked Ella if Mother wasn't feeling well.

"She seems to have something on her mind." Answered Ella.

"What is it? She never said exactly. But I believe she'd be better satisfied if you'd leave the restaurant."

"Sure!"

***

Three months passed, and Sue had been home four times. Twice she called out and told Theodore he need not come for her. Oh, yes, she was well, getting along just fine. Business was rushing. She would attend some church in town.

Dear Sue, Mother wrote:

We sure miss you so, when you don't come home on Sundays. Next Sunday we are having Fred's over, and Uncle Tim and all his family from Illinois will be here. Can't you

come home? Someone took me by the hand yesterday and said,
I am praying for your daughter these days. You must know how
I am concerned about your spiritual life. 'Pride goeth before
destruction and a haughty spirit before a fall.'

Lovingly, Mother

Sue bit her lips. She tore the letter into fine bits and threw them into the wastebasket. Mr. Webb caught her arm.

"Did you get a letter you did not like, Susie dear?"

"Well, I did not like the last of it." Her pretty eyes snapped. Oh, how cute she was when she acted like that, and Mr. Webb told her so.

"Tell me all about it." She shook her head.

"Tell me from whom it was."

"My mother", she replied softly.

"Oh", he laughed, "does she want you to come home?"

"Next Sunday, I really ought to. My uncle from Illinois is coming."

"You can go if you want to."

"I can?"

"If you'll be sure to come back. We couldn't get along without you now, little Susie, and you know it, don't you?"

She only smiled.

"What did your mother say? Tell me." Someone came in. She shook her head.

"Pride goeth before destruction and a haughty spirit—" the words tormented her. "Haughty spirit!" Oh, how dare mother say she was haughty? Why, that means ugly, overbearing pride. She wanted to forget it. The bits of paper were in the basket, but the verse remained. Sue tried to be sweet to the people who came in. Several times she forgot part of the orders and had to ask the second time. She was heartily ashamed of herself. The other girls whispered and exchanged glances.

"Pride goeth before—before destruction." She glanced in the mirrors as she passed and sighed. She would take time off at noon to get her hair set. Once that morning she thought that Mr. Webb looked displeased. She needed new slippers and would get some if she had to charge them.

"Pride goeth before—" Over and over those words flashed before Sue as she waited on tables that evening. Her feet hurt, and her head ached. She hadn't been so tired for a long time. Once she thought of happy evenings at home when Mother popped corn, and they all went to bed early. Sue dropped a plate. Every eye in the restaurant was on her. She tried to smile and pick up the bits quickly, but instead her eyes filled with tears. The other girls smiled, and Mr. Webb snapped his finger at them. He called Sue to his desk.

"Listen, Little Girl." He said in an under-tone, "you're tired tonight; you go home to your rooming place. You rest a little, and then get dressed up—see—and I will be by for you about ten."

Sue's mouth fell open. She looked half frightened. "Why?"

"I'm going to take you out riding; I need a little change myself. Now, you go on, and do as I say. Honey! We'll both forget our troubles, for a while, at least."

Sue left the restaurant without saying more, and the other girls exchanged wise glances.

Mrs. Matthews met Sue at the door. "What has gone wrong, Sue? Are you sick?"

"Oh, no, Mrs. Matthews, she smiled. "I'm going out for a ride."

"I see." Mrs. Matthews looked surprised.

"I never heard of Mr. Webb letting one of his girls off early for a date."

"He told me he was coming to take me out for a ride."

"Sue Smith!" Cried Mrs. Matthews. The paper in her hand fell to the floor.

"What?"

"Mr. Webb! You mean to tell me you are having a date with Mr. Webb!"

"Just going for a ride."

"Sue Smith!" Mrs. Matthews grabbed Sue by the arm. "Do you realize what you are doing? Do you know that man?"

"He's awfully nice to work for and he has treated me swell."

"Maybe too swell! Listen child, have you been out with him before?"

"He has often brought me home. That's all." Sue was visibly irritated. Mrs. Mathews had never spoken like this to her before.

"Why he has a wife and no telling how many lady friends. If you start running around with Mr. Webb you cannot room here. And no mincing words about that! What do you suppose your parents would say to this?"

Sue looked down. "Pride goeth before destruction."

The words seemed to be printed all over the wall, "and a haughty spirit before—"

"I know they wouldn't approve of it, at all. Continued Mrs. Matthews; it is in complete conflict with your faith; I know that. I am a Catholic and we do not believe in divorce or adultery either. And I know your people do not either. I am totally shocked beyond all words. You know a lot better than that, Sue! You have been brought up different than me. I know that; and if you go astray I'm not responsible for your choices. I suppose your parents are very worried about you, even that you had a room here with me. I have seen you slipping in some things, and I have a big notion to write to your mother and let her know what all you've been up to. I am sure she is a good woman. I have never once tried to interfere with your choices, have I?"

"No." Sue's face became flushed. Her lips trembled.

"No, and I won't either. I respect your parents and their devotion to their faith, and I'd respect you a lot more, Sue, if you'd choose to be more true to yourself."

Sue's eyes were filled with tears now. She fell into the nearest chair.

"You have no idea, Sue, how people watch you people who claim to be Christians, and especially the girls coming from a home like yours. I have even prayed in my own heart, that you will be able to stop before you go any further. Years ago, I hired one of your people, a girl by the name of Mary Miller; She worked for me a while; and she certainly was not ashamed of her religion! I always admired her, too. She used to tell me a lot of things about the Bible, and I only wished I could believe as she did too. She married a fine man young man of her own faith, and I heard that he became a preacher. It was a beautiful faith that girl had."

Sue wiped a big tear from both eyes. Mrs. Matthews went on.

"I am very, very sorry Sue, that you would let a man like Mr. Webb overpower you like this. You are a precious innocent girl caught in his trap."

Sue thought— "pride goeth before destruction."

"Of course you can do as you like, but, if you go out with Mr. Webb, I'm going to call your mother on the phone and tell her. He will ruin you, and that is not all!"

"Pride goeth before destruction—destruction—and the spirit before the fall."

"This may seem like plain speaking, Sue, but I feel like saying it. You are still young, and pretty, and have a happy future before you."

"I must let the Lord lead. That's it Mrs. Matthews. My brother said when I came to town—" Sue did not finish. She was crying. Mrs. Matthews let her cry.

"You won't feel bad towards me for talking like this to you, will you? Will you Sue?"

"No, Oh No! Oh, I see it now. I used to be a real Christian, but "Pride goeth before the destruction. It all started with me a few years ago."

"When my mother wrote that to me in a letter and it almost made me furious," confessed Sue softly. "It is true though."

"True?" True for sure! I know of two girls in this very town who ran around with Mr. Webb and they have very few friends anymore."

"Oh, Mrs. Matthews, I did not know!"

"Well, Sue, they probably did not know either; but you said "Pride goeth before." They were nice girls and used to attend Sunday school at the church across the street.

Without another word, Sue walked to the phone and called home.

"Hello Mother, is Theodore there? Tell him to call me at Mrs. Matthews tonight any time."

"When Mr. Webb calls, Mrs. Matthews you tell him that I went home and that I gave up my job. Many thanks for all you have done for me." An hour later, Sue was on her way home.

"You say you gave up your job Sue?" Asked Theodore after they got in the car.

"Yes. I did."

"What happened?"

"Oh—Sue hesitated. "I thought I'd better before—before the fall. I've been proud, and—haughty—and I—I want to begin all over, Theodore, and let God lead."

Nothing Covered

By Christmas Carol Kauffman, age 38, Hannibal, Missouri
Originally published September 8 and 15, 1940
in the Youth's Christian Companion

Agnes swung the one foot that dangled. The other one was curled up under her on the arm of the fireside chair. She bit the eraser on the end of her yellow pencil. She looked at the floor and sighed.

"Agnes!" The woman just around the corner of the dining room dropped the overalls she was mending. She dropped them into her lap.

"Did you want me Mother?" Agnes was beside her now.

"I just wondered why that big sigh I heard in there." The woman smiled up into the face of her girl. They looked more like sisters than mother and daughter.

Agnes gave another longer and louder sigh, and sat down. For a moment she just sat.

"Well, I'll just tell you, Mother," she started, "I'm really up against it this time."

"What do you mean, Agnes?" Now, any mother might have asked the same question. Mrs. Davidson's eyes opened wide. She had never heard Agnes make such a statement in just that tone of voice, and with such a look of despair—no, not in eighteen years.

"Well, I'm supposed to write a story for English Composition," she began.

"Yes." Mrs. Davidson rethreaded her needle.

"But, Mother, I don't have any, and I can't get any." She folded her arms tightly across her waist. "The more I try to think the blanker I get." She scratched her arm nervously.

Mother smiled in spite of the forlorn look on the girl's face. "What kind of story are you to write?"

"Well, it's to be a true story and one that teaches some moral lesson." Agnes rolled the yellow pencil back and forth across her papers and looked serious. She couldn't think straight.

"A true story?"

"Yes, Mother, an actual happening, that's just what Mr. Glade said. He said it has to have a solid kernel of truth, you know what I mean. It teaches a moral. It should or could be an actual happening, or it must at least seem probable."

"Now that's what?" Mother winked and continued stitching the striped patch on Bobbie's overall knee.

"Don't tease me Mother; I'm really in earnest over this! I'm nearly frantic about this assignment. It's no joke. These stories have to be in by tomorrow when school ends and I haven't even started yet, because I haven't even a little idea about what to write about. Elsie and Jane handed their stories in already, and I'm nowhere even close to starting."

Agnes was on her feet now, walking back and forth in front of the buffet.

"Why, Mother," Agnes stopped, having a hand on one hip dramatically, "I surely don't think it would be easy to sit and write out stories. I used to think you could almost roll them out like cookie dough and cut some of them into hearts and some into stars and others chickens and fix some up with sugar and some with raisins and some with cinnamon and bake them and pass them out and, Mother, it is absolutely not true!" It's not that easy, I tell you!"

Mrs. Davidson had to throw her head back and laugh in spite of herself. Agnes didn't laugh.

"When you were a young thing, Agnes, you would tell all kinds of different stories to Bobby by the hour. You would make them up as fast as you could talk; one after another without even trying."

"Well, maybe so then. But what kind of stories were they? Animals that talked, and flowers that smiled and rivers that laughed and all kinds of fantastic probabilities. That wild imagination I had then does not help me out now. I want a solid kernel of truth."

She pounded her fist on the buffet and looked at her mother straight in her eyes. They were deep blue like her own.

"I want a story that is true, that actually happened, or one that will happen. I want one that has no impossibilities or inabilities in it. I want something real, and true to life that teaches a lesson." She hurried on.

"Now, Mr. Glade suggested in class: You sow what you reap."

"What?" Mrs. Davidson Tried not to smile. "Oh, you know what I mean. I'm so—stupid, Mother. I know- You reap what you sow. Now that's a solid kernel of truth. It's a truth and no one can deny it. Now, Agnes Glade, read a story that tells us that 'love never fails." It's another solid kernel of truth that he illustrated. 'Be sure your sins will find you out.' is another one. There are lots and lots of truths to wrap a story around, but I just can't find any, it seems. I want something real! —oh, Mother, I—"

The girl's voice faltered. She bent slowly toward the buffet and her slender body slumped.

"Prayer changes things," ventured Mother. "I guess that's another truth, isn't it?"

"Why, Agnes. I never saw you so upset over your school work. Did all the others in your class have this much of a hard time too?"

"I don't know; I never asked. I was not going to admit to any others that I'm having a hard time."

"Must it be a Bible truth?" Asked Mother.

"Not necessarily. He read us a story about 'rolling stones gather no moss.' That's a term I don't for sure understand. Then he also read us a story about a man who borrowed a pulley from a friend and while he was using it, it got cracked. But he returned it and never mentioned the crack. Also one about a man who, he and his neighbor were both putting up ice, and the man who borrowed the pulley really hoped it would break while the neighbor used it so he could get ahead while the ice season was on. They lived twenty miles from town. Well, the story went on to reveal the man thoughts. It was awful how he pretended to be his best friend, and in his heart wished he had a misfortune. Then a few days after he returned the pulley, this man's son was over watching him put up ice. And they were pulling a 250-pound cake of ice and the pulley broke and flew back and hit the back of the man's own son's head. The boy spent a long time hanging between life and death, and this man sold several cows and several horses to pay the doctor bills. Finally the boy got well, but he never was right after that. The man himself nearly lost his own mind over it, and finally, after years of heartbreaking trials, he confessed to his neighbor his selfish, wicked thoughts toward him."

"And then what?" Asked Mother.

"Well, Mr. Glade asked the class to name the truth taught in that story."

"What is it?" Mrs. Davidson looked up.

"He got several answers from the class, but the truth is this: If you dig a pit for someone else to fall into, you're likely to fall into it yourself."

"That's often true too." Mrs. Davidson folded Bobbie's overalls slowly and stuck the needle in her dress.

"Can't you think of any story, Agnes?"

"I've tried to think until my head hurts. I've been wondering, and searching, and groping and—and struggling, for a solid worthwhile kernel of—"

Knock! Knock!

Agnes answered the knock. In the doorway stood Sandy Hornback, cap in hand. He evidently had been running, for his breath came in bunches as he spoke.

"Miss Agnes," he said, "Mom wants ter know if you kin come over ter our house an' take ker of the chiluns whiles she goes ter the doctor orfice fer my dad?"

"Is he sick?"

"Yes'um. An Doc Hornback ain't no kin to us if he does have our name, an' he won't come out ter the house 'hout the cash ter hand him, an' we ain't got it; so Mom has ter go down to his office ter get medicine, 'an Mom is sceared to hav me mind Joe and Annabell an' the twins besides Dad, fer he's orful sick, Miss Agnes, an' I got ter hurry back. Can you come and what shall I tell Mom?" He was backing away from the door as he spoke.

"Well, yes, of course, I'll be right over, Sandy. Do you live—?"

"Same ole' place, Miss Agnes you know."

"Yes, I know. Up over the old wagon factory?" She called out.

"Yes'um; that's the place," and off he ran putting his cap on as he ran.

"Agnes, you haven't had your supper." Mother was on her feet now.

"Never mind, Mother. I must go. I'm not hungry anyway."

"But, who was that boy?" Mrs. Davidson followed Agnes to the door.

"Why, He's my newest pupil in my Sunday School class. Snappy brought him last Sunday, but I really found him myself and told Snappy to bring him." She was gone.

***

The old stairs of Sandy's home creaked and snapped as Agnes ran up. A peculiar odor of wood ashes, burnt potatoes, half-dried wash, and oil of herbs, greeted her as the door opened. Sandy was sitting on a box beside the iron bed. It was painted blue. It was little Joe who graciously opened the door for Miss Agnes. He smiled up at her with a brave, shy smile which meant, "Come in," The twins both in blue jean overalls were sitting in the corner of the second room (there were but two) nibbling at dry, cold biscuits , and Annabelle was standing on a little stool with both hands in a dishpan of cold, greasy water. The man on the bed did not open his eyes. He was moaning with every breath. Agnes stood close and touched Sandy gently on the shoulder.

"What's wrong with your father?"

"The boy shrugged his shoulders. "Search me, Miss Agnes."

"How long has he been sick?"

"Since last night. He comed home from the work sick, an' couldn't eat nothin'fer supper atall."

"Was he ever like this before?"

"Not as I know of. Mom don't know what ter feed him or what ter do fer him, an' Dad he jes' won't talk none, only groans thata way."

Agnes felt his head. It was hot. "I wish I knew what to do until your mother gets back. I'm not much good around sick folks. I would hardly make a nurse, but I am a real good hand at washing dishes."

So saying, Agnes crossed the room and patted the little girl who was still blankly staring at her and soaking her hands in the cold dishwater.

"Let me do these dishes for you, little sister. What say?"

Annabell needed no urging to get off her little perch. Her smile of gratitude was sufficient for Agnes to realize how welcome her offer was to this eight-year-old. She put the dishpan on the oil stove and talked to the twins until the water was hot again.

"And you're not going to tell me your names?" They only stared at Agnes in dumb amazement.

"Is it Dannie or Davie?" she ventured quietly.

"Oh, no'um," spoke up Annabell, twisting the hem of her dress around her finger. "They're girls."

"I beg your pardon. I thought—well, what are their names, Sister? You tell me if they won't."

"June and Judy. They was borned on Daddy's birthday." Smiled Annabell.

"Wasn't that nice?" Agnes patted their curly heads.

She walked to the foot of the iron bed. The man was still moaning. Poor Sandy looked bewildered. Joe, who was small for his age leaned hard against the wall behind Sandy and swallowed and swallowed.

"I'll wash the dishes." Whispered Agnes to Sandy, "and if there's anything I can do you call me." He nodded.

The dishes were washed and wiped. Agnes lit a kerosene lamp and would have swept the floor, too, but could find no broom.

"Come here June and Judy," Agnes held out both arms.

"Let me hold you two on my lap." Without voicing objection or consent, they were soon upon her.

Half an hour later Mrs. Hornock ran up the steps pale and breathless. She rushed straight to the bed and bending over the man patted his face and stroked his hair. "Ed," she said gently, "Ed, oh Ed, listen to me, Ed. I've got some medicine here for you. Get some water please, Miss, out o' the pail over there. Just bring the dipper. Ed, open your mouth just a little."

The man only moaned and shook his head.

"Why Ed," choked the woman frantically. "Won't you take it for now, since I went an fetched it?" Feebly the man shook his head.

"But Ed, you must. It will help you." Again, the man feebly shook his head.

"Try it, Ed. Come on, jes' open yer lips a little. Please, Ed," she coaxed.

"No-—use." His voice was thick.

"Ed, please," she cried. The man on the bed slowly raised one hand. His voice was a throaty whisper.

"Yes, Ed." The woman caught his hand in both of hers and bent over him. Sandy, Joe, Annabell and the twins clustered around the foot of the bed in strange fright. The one oil lamp cast a long dark shadow across the room. Agnes gripped the dipper.

"Kitty," he repeated. "Bill—ain't dead."

"What?" The woman half screamed and clutched the man's hand. "What's that, Ed?" She bent over him until her face almost touched his. She shook him. The perspiration dropped from his forehead.

"Bill—ain't—ain't—"

"Bill ain't dead? Ed—you mean Bill Theason? What?"

Ed gave a loud moan and shook all over. A strange rattle came from his throat.

"Are you talkin out o' your head, Ed?" She shook him. She took both hands and shook him again.

"I—I—saw Bill." He choked.

"When?" she demanded.

"Yester—"

"Yesterday? Where? Where'd you see Bill? Oh Ed, it's just crazy; I know it."

"Kitty, I—saw Bill, an—an—by—by, Kitty," he whispered.

"Ed, Ed!" screamed the woman. "No—no—Ed, answer me.!" She shook him madly.

"Answer me, Ed. You mean Bill Theason—my Bill? Oh, oh!"

The woman dropped on her knees beside the bed and clutched the lifeless man.

"Oh—my God! What's wrong?" And she crumpled to a heap on the floor.

"Oh, Sandy," cried Agnes. "Here, take this dipper. Put some on her face quick, Sandy."

Agnes gathered the woman into her arms and dragged her to the only chair in the room. She shook until her teeth chattered. The woman was not large, but it took all of the girl's strength to lift her.

"There, there, Mrs. Hornback. Just rest your head on my arms; you'll soon feel better. Hold her on that side, Sandy. There! Let Anabell take the water."

The woman partly opened her eyes. "Are—are you Sandy's teacher?"

"Yes, Ma'am." Agnes stroked her arm.

"An', did—did you hear him," she pointed towards the bed, "Did you hear him say Bill ain't dead or was I hearing things? Did you?"

"Yes, that's what he said. Who is Bill?"

"Oh, lady, why Bill Theason was—"

The woman caught her breath and looked up. So did Agnes. There was a gentle knock on the banister in the hall. Sandy went to the door. In the semidarkness stood a middle aged man, hat in hand.

"Is this where Ed Hornback lives, my boy?" He asked.

"Yes, sir," answered Sandy.

The woman on the chair stopped breathing for a moment. Agnes felt her arms get stiff and prickly with goose hide.

"Is your mother here, my boy?"

"Yes, Sir," answered Sandy softly.

"And may I see her please?"

"Well," Sandy hesitated. "Well, sir—a—step inside. Mom, jes fainted a bit ago 'cause—" Sandy's voice broke. Great tears stood in his eyes and they blinded him.

The man stepped inside. For a moment the room seemed to sway. The man staggered a few steps forward. He grabbed the table for support. He leaned forward and looked at the woman.

"Katharine," he whispered.

The woman on the chair did not answer. Her mouth fell open, but no words came out.

"Katharine," repeated the man, bending forward and shading his eyes with his hand.

"Bill," she whispered. "Bill, you—you isn't dead?" Her pale face got whiter.

"Dead? Dead? Who told you I was dead?" He muttered hoarsely.

"Why Ed did. Bill, I thought all these ten years, you were dead! Ed told me you died in France. I—I believed him. Ed said yer dyin' request was fer him to come home and take me and Sandy an—an so we got married. Why Bill, Bill," she cried.

"Where's Ed?" Bill's hand dropped on the table with a thud.

The woman pointed to the bed in the corner. The man inched across the room until he reached the iron bed.

"Ed, how about this?" Silence.

"Ed," repeated the man louder. No answer. Not even a moan.

The man looked at the woman, then at Sandy, then at the motionless form of the man on the bed. He looked and he looked.

"Is he?" He asked turning to the woman.

"Is he?" She asked him. "Oh, Bill is he really—really dead, do you think?"

The man on the floor looked at the man on the bed for several minutes. The clock on the dresser ticked on and on before he spoke.

"Katherine," he said coming back to where she still sat. "I met Ed yesterday down town; first I've seen him since he landed in New York ten years ago. I knowed him an' he knowed me. But he acted so strange—not glad t' see me. I couldn't understand. He asked me what I did after we parted in New York. I told him I stopped off in Pennsylvania to see my mother. She was makin' a quilt fer Sandy's little bed, an' she told me if I'd stay around about two more days, she could finish it fer me to take along home an' surprise my wife. So I did. I told him how I started for home an'—" the man stopped abruptly. A great lump came into his throat.

"Bill," the woman leaned forward. "Bill, then what?"

"Then what?" He swallowed hard. "You know what then. That note." He held out one trembling hand.

"What note? Bill? What note?" The woman on the chair got to her feet. She stood for a moment. She staggered toward him she would have touched him, but he was back behind her.

"You know, Katherine. That note you left with Mrs. Clark next door?"

"I know nothin' of it. Bill, I don't know what you mean. I left no note. How would I? Why should I? Ed said you were dead. I left with him the next day. He said that's what you wanted me to do. We went back to Montana right away."

"Katharine, you mean you did not write that note tellin' me you were through with me forever? He shouted.

"Why, Bill, Bill! God knows I did not say I was through with you? Oh, Bill, I always loved you!" I was heartbroken when I heard that you were dead." She held her breath for a moment. "I believed Ed all these years and never knowed different." Great tears blinded her. "Oh, Bill, and you are married too? I have Joe and Anabell and the twins. Are you married too?" She wrung her hands.

"What if I said yes?" He answered.

"Oh, Bill! He saw her sway. He caught her in his arms.

"But, I'm not Katherine. I'm not. Look at me dear, I'm not."

He kissed her. "I trusted you. I loved you. When I read the note it almost killed me, Katherine." He held her.

"But how did you find me here?" She asked.

"Well, when I met Ed, I told him I would go along home with him fer a meal. I said it in a joking way. He acted so queer. I asked him if he was married and he said he had five children. I told him that I never married but was searching for my wife and boy every day. I told him about my empty house, and about being invited over to get the note you left."

"Mrs. Clark told me about some strange man brought it over and left it there. I thought I couldn't believe it."

"Katherine," he held her out at arm's length and looked in her face earnestly, Tell me once more, didn't you write that note?"

"I did not Bill. I tell you, I never knew anyone took a note to Mrs. Clark." She looked so earnest that he had to believe her.

"Was it?" Bill Theason walked over to the man on the iron bed and pointed to the man and said, "Did you do that Ed Hornback? You need not answer me. You can give your answer to God almighty!"

"Listen, Katherine, Listen; yesterday when I told Ed I was searchin' fer my wife an' son, he got white as a sheet. I couldn't understand. I never, ever suspected such a thing. Katherine, did you ever love him? Did he ever really ever truly love you? Tell me!"

"Several years before I met you, he tried to convince me—" I did love him for these last ten years, because he was good to me, most always; but I always loved you! But, I was lonesome fer you. But I loved you, Bill; it's you I've always loved! I was so lonesome fer you!" she sobbed.

"Well, yesterday when I was atalkin' to Ed, he got so white and just stared at me for a long, long time, and finally said, 'Well, Bill, I'll get out o' the way.' Just like that he said it."

"Katherine, do you think—?"

"Oh, Bill, do you really s'pose oh, he came home last night—so sick. I didn't know what to do or think, or say—oh Ed." Katherine Hornback shook with uncontrollable sobs.

"Don't Katherine dear," she felt one strong gentle arm around her. With the other, Bill Theason drew Sandy close to him. Wide-eyed and trembling the boy allowed himself to be drawn close.

"Sandy, my boy," spoke the man tenderly, "life is stranger than fiction. When I was a boy like you, my mother took me to a Sunday school. I learned a scripture verse there that goes like this: There is nothing covered that will not be revealed—Neither hid that shall not be known. When I was a young man I took the Lord as my Savior." The man's lips quivered and it was hard for him to control his voice.

"I served my mother's God fer several years; an then went back into sin. I joined the army. I was called to go to France when you were just a baby. Some day, I'll tell you the whole story of how I grieved the good Lord. I wasn't more an' over there till the armistice was signed and I came home. My

God!" His arms tightened around the woman, He shook with sobs. "What grief" he choked, "has been my portion these past years! Two weeks ago I stumbled I stumbled in ta a mission. I was so cold and hungry and lonesome fer ya both. That there verse I learned when I was a youngster in Sunday school, the preacher used it sorta as a text. I listened—I drank it in, and I got and found a new faith that there night, and somehow when I prayed so, so hard, I found me a faith that night, that somehow, somewhere, sometime, God would find you fer me, I began to pray real, real hard, with all the faith I could muster up. I had prayed and prayed many a times fer you and your sweet mama—but I was also so bitter, an, even so, I found somehow the strong arms of Jesus around me then, an somehow I found God where I had left off, where I lefted Him, an somehow someway love just came inta my brokenup heart —and pure love came inta my heart for you and your sweet mama."

"Oh, Katherine, my darlin, have you been a takin these here children to Sunday school?" He looked lovingly down on her. She shook her head.

"Oh, I started last Sunday," whispered Sandy, looking up into the man's face. "That's my teacher." He pointed to Agnes in the shadow of the stove,

"Oh!" Somehow he hadn't had time yet to notice her there. "I see," he said.

"Miss, I hadn't noticed ya, or I was too much filled with excitement ta notice ya. You've heard some strange things here in this house tonight, but good sister, whatever ya do," he held her hand, "be-a real, real teacher ta my boy, an' teach the Word of God, fer you'll never know what just one verse'll do and may mean ta a young boy. It sure meant somthin to me. The Bible's true sista, there's nothing covered that shall not be—"

Knock; Knock.

Bill Theason went to the door.

"Is Agnes Davidson here?"

"Yes, Bobbie", answered Agnes.

"Well, Mom said I should come to walk home with you. It's dark now and nearly eight-thirty."

"All right, I guess I'm ready unless—"

"I'll see after things, Miss. And thank you."

"Theason bowed to her with gratitude.

"I'll be back in the morning, Mrs. Hornback. I'll be glad to do anything to help you."

"Thanks, Miss Agnes," called Sandy. "Please come back."

At two o'clock Mrs. Davidson woke out of a deep sleep. She heard Agnes cough. She sat up in bed and listened. She heard steps above her.

"Agnes." She stood outside her door. He hand was on the knob.

"Why, Mother." Agnes opened the door.

"Agnes, what are you doing?"

"Mother, I have been writing. Come in. I'm on the very last sentence."

In The Flower Shop

By Christmas Carol Kauffman, age 40, Hannibal, Missouri
Originally published March 29 and April 5, 1942

In a single dismal basement room, under Shad Temple's
Pet Store, lived Granny Galesburg and Sally Ann. Just those
two, and no more, for Sally Ann was all Granny had left any
more. It was three months since Granny's son had died—
Homer, her precious and only child. Homer, so handsome, so
robust and dependable, was gone!

It seemed like a bad dream that she and Sally Ann had
had, and that some morning they would just have to wake up
and see him and her talking. There on the wall hung his striped
work suit he had on the morning he had come home all doubled
up with pain in his side. There it hung so limp and silent.
Granny touched it every day, and so did Sally Ann. They
couldn't bear to put it away yet. But some day she meant to
when Sally was outside. She'd fold it tenderly; Granny would,
and put it in the bottom of the old trunk with Elizabeth's dress.

Somehow the three of them Granny, Homer, and Sally
Ann, had been used to getting along without Elizabeth, for she

had not lived to see Sally Ann walk. Granny had to be Sally Ann's mother and grandmother all in one. But now she had to be her mother and grandmother and father – no—no she could never be a father to Sally Ann—never!

He was so energetic and strong. The truth of this possibility—the cruel truth made Granny suddenly grow old. Her hair had been white as long as Sally Ann could remember, but her face was young and sunny, and Granny could smile through most anything as long as Homer came home every night and called her mother. But it was different now.

Never again to be called mother! Your only child gone! For Sally Ann's sake Granny Galesburg braced up, but in spite of her determination to stay young, her steps were getting slower and slower and her white hair was getting even whiter. That extra bed, that extra chair, that extra plate and cup, the striped work suit, all made the already dismal room more dismal. Sunbeams seldom came in that basement room, even on the brightest days.

Sally Ann could play in the alley sometimes if Granny sat on Mrs. Dunkin's steps and watched for trucks. It wasn't safe for Sally Ann to play there without a watchman. Once a day when the weather was fit, Sally Ann would go up to the "front" as she called it, and look at the pets in Shad's store window.

There were dogs of every description: black ones, white ones, brown ones, spotted ones, slick ones with thin legs, shaggy ones with bigger legs, fluffy ones, long ones, short ones. There were kittens of every kind; white rats with pink eyes; birds, singing birds, talking birds, birds that chattered, birds that screeched, birds that just hopped around, and some that only sat and loved each other. And there were other queer little creatures Sally Ann didn't know the names of. How Sally Ann liked to stand on the walk and watch the little pups roll around in the clean straw.

Whenever Granny gave permission, Sally Ann would go down the street and block to Crescent's Flower Shop. Nothing pleased her more. To Sally Ann the flowers were far more fascinating than the pets. The velvet faces seemed to speak to her in the huge plate-glass windows, and tell happy stories about the beautiful garden her mother and father had gone to. She remembered hearing the lady sing at her father's funeral. Then the minister said something about lilies too, but she didn't remember what it was, except every time she asked Granny, Granny began to cry and draw her close to her and said, "Oh, honey child, you dear little girl, wasn't it all beautiful, so beautiful!" Then shake so hard with sobs that Sally Ann hated to hear it again. She didn't want to know.

There were so many things Sally did want to know about: those beautiful flowers in the shop window; where they all came from; what their names were; how much they cost. Sally Ann saw well-dressed women go inside, but Granny had often told her not to for some reason.

It was the second week in April. She and Granny were eating their simple supper of potato soup, when Sally Ann looked up and said: "Granny."

"Yes, Honey."

"How many days till your birthday?" A cloud crossed Granny's face.

"Why, child, what made you think of that?"

"Well, don't you remember the last time on your birthday, Daddy bringed you a present all wrapped up in pretty green paper?"

Sally Ann took another spoonful of soup and looked up. Granny gave a big sigh and dropped her hands. Did she remember? How could she not forget it?

"Don't you remember, Granny?" asked Sally Ann earnestly.

"Yes, honey child, I remember." She spoke to Granny very softly.

"Well, how many days yet before it comes? – your birthday I mean." A cloud crossed Granny's face. Sally Ann bent forward.

"My birthday will be on Sunday, pet."

"And what is today?" Sally swallowed.

"Today is Tuesday. But what—and why do you think of my birthday, Child?"

"Because of the lilies in the Flower Shop, Granny."

"Don't you remember? Your birthday always comes when the Lilies are best."

"Today the windows are full of them and Daddy bringed home some for you last time, remember? Remember Granny?"

Granny Galesburg could not swallow the lump in her throat or keep the tears from blinding her eyes. There would be super presents from Homer. Now the pension was scarcely enough to pay the rent and feed them. And in a few years Sally Ann would be going away, off to school.

"Don't cry, Granny." Sally Ann said bravely. "If Daddy could, he'd get some this time too, wouldn't he, Granny?" Her blue eyes opened wide. Granny spoke slowly.

"You just loved it, didn't you?"

"My, yes indeed, I loved it!" Her voice was very low now.

"Why do they have so many in the window of the Flower Shop? Oh, Granny, today, I saw more than a hundred in there, really there were, I am sure. Some had red and goldish paper around them, and some had purple and silver paper all tied on with pretty ribbons. Oh, say Granny, I never saw so many different ones. Do lots of people have birthdays on Sunday like you?"

"Sunday is Easter, Honey Pet. My birthday is on Easter this year."

"Those are Easter Lilies."

"What does Easter mean Granny?" Her blue eyes opened wide.

"That's when Jesus Christ rose from the dead. That's what I learned when I was a little girl. But please don't start asking me any more question, 'cause I jes don't know how to answer them. There's lots of things I don't know. But I do know I'm going to have a birthday this comin' Sunday, and the calendar says it will be Easter; an you're five years old and I am going to be seventy." Grandma stopped suddenly.

"Do you know anyone who could tell us about Easter? I want to know Granny. About, you know Granny, about Jesus, an' wakin' from the dead, an'all."

Granny Galesburg sat for several moments with her hand on her face. She seemed to be in deep, deep thought.

"Could you, Granny?" repeated Sally Ann. She sat up on one knee and leaned on Granny's leg. She could hear her heart pound within her entire body. Never before had Sally Ann put such a question to her. Her two bright eyes pierced her very soul. They both wanted to know. They had the right to know. All at once Granny saw Homer, her precious baby's face shine out of Sally Ann's. Once, years ago, thirty years ago, she was asked almost the very same thing and she ignored him and laughed him off, and told him go just go and play with the other boys outside. The light is his eyes somehow caught her attention. He was called "home" so suddenly. The last hours he had suffered so and no one could talk to him. Granny didn't have time to really think until after he was gone.

Did Sally Ann suspect and conceive of the gnawing of Granny's soul these last few months? There was way more than mere loneliness that made her steps much slower, her hair whiter and her smiles fewer? Once Homer had wanted to also know what Easter meant, and she hurriedly told him she'd some how find out.

Over the years, Granny Galesburg had told herself she knew what it was all about. She wished she knew. She could not read, and was too ashamed to ask. A number of times she had been invited to church by a neighbor and she would always make the excuse that Sally Ann needed to take her nap, or that she was too tired to go herself. Now Sally Ann would soon be old enough to know for herself and want to know who Jesus Christ was, and—and Granny's poor head ached and she tugged nervously at her apron bib.

"Do you know Granny?" repeated Sally Ann, as she put her spoon on the table.

"Well, I'll tell you, Sally Ann. If you had a pretty dress to wear and since you're too young to send you off to Sunday School, I guess I could come along and learn all them things too." Sally Ann looked wistfully down over her sadly faded print dress.

That night she lay awake while Granny slept. She had never prayed, for no one had ever taught her how, but her childish innocent soul cried out to some unknown immortal being; and when she did finally fall asleep, she dreamed she was inside the Flower Shop standing among these exquisite lilies, touching them—smelling them—and behind one tall plant stood a man with a shining celestial countenance. He smiled at her for a moment, and then disappeared.

She woke with a start. Granny was still breathing heavily. In the early dawn, she could see her father's striped suit hanging on the wall beside her. She reached out and touched it.

"Oh, Daddy," she whispered, half sobbing; "oh, Daddy, tell me how I can get Granny one of those pretty flowers. I haven't a penny, and I can't leave Granny to go and work, cause I'm way to young and I haven't nothin' to sell. It would make her so happy to have one on her birthday, Daddy." And Sally Ann fell asleep. It was after eight when she opened her eyes. She sat up in bed and rubbed them with her little fists.

"You must have been dreaming, honey pet," Granny was bending over her and stroking her forehead gently.

"Oh, I was, Granny." She smiled…

"Oh, no—I—oh, I wish it would come true. Oh, Granny, it was the bestest dream I ever had. Something you'd like, I know. But I don't want to tell yet. Not till…." She clapped her hand over her mouth. Sally Ann chuckled as she dressed herself.

"Can I go to the Flower Shop?"

"What for, Sally Ann?"

"To look in the windows."

"It's raining," came Granny's answer.

"It is? Oh! And it's turning to snow. Don't go out in the wet. Your little shoes are way to thin!"

It snowed all morning. By noon a young blizzard had started. Sally Ann tried to content herself with her paper dolls and laughed to herself as she sipped her imaginary tea.

***

By Saturday, most of the snow had disappeared. The weather had moderated considerably, and Granny told Sally Ann she could walk down to the Flower Shop if she didn't stay long. She put on her little short red coat and hurried down the street.

"Oh!" Sally Ann gave an exclamation of disappointment when she reached the Flower Shop window. Most of the lilies were gone! "One—two—three—four." Sally Ann stood on her tip toes and counted ten plants.

Her little heart beat faster and faster. She hurried over to the edge of the cement walk and looked in the gutter. Her heart sank. There was nothing there. She looked again. Up and down the front of the Flower Shop walked Sally Ann. Her lips quivered. Tears blinded her eyes. She looked back to the plants in the window. The clerk was selling two more out of the window. Now there were only eight left. Sally Ann stood wistfully watching the lady come out with a lily in each arm.

"Hi, Curly Top." Sally Ann looked up startled. A man had his hand on her head, patting her gently. Sally Ann did not speak. The man was a stranger to her.

"Pretty head of hair you got, little sister," he said, still patting her soft brown curls.

"How much will you take for one of them?" He smiled down at her. Sally Ann looked up, but did not answer. She was frightened.

"I say," went on the man, "Will you sell me your curls? They are mighty pretty, they are, —and see—" he took off his hat and laughed, "See how bald I am!" Still Sally Ann was too astonished to answer. She was still frightened. The man laughed, and staggered down the street and entered a saloon.

Sally Ann stood as if her feet were frozen to the side walk. Suddenly a new idea seized her. She turned quickly and waked as fast as her feet would take her, until she reached Tom's Barber Shop. She entered shyly and closed the door slowly. Her breath came in big bunches, and her cheeks burned. An old man was in the chair, and a young man was waiting his turn.

"Hello, girlie," said the barber pleasantly as the door closed behind her.

"Hello", answered Sally Ann.

"What can I do for you today, little miss?" The barber held his scissors in midair.

Sally Ann shifted from one foot to the other. She held her hands in her red coat pockets, and then shaking her curly head, she began,

"Oh, sir, I—I want to sell my curls."

"Sell your curls? Who told you that I would buy your hair?"

"Oh, don't you ever buy a person's hair? Ever?" She looked disappointed. She bit her lip. The barber's voice was not harsh, but somehow she was almost afraid of him. He looked very tall in his white coat.

"Why do you want to sell your beautiful curls?" The old man in the chair sat up straight.

"Why—why," faltered Sally Ann, "You know my Granny?"

"No, I don't." The barber shook his head.

"Well, My Granny, she's got a birthday tomorrow, you know, an' an' my Daddy can't get her one of them lilies this time, 'cause—'cause—" she was twisting the corner of her little red coat now and a big tear stood in each blue eye.

"Cause why?" He still held the scissors high.

"Cause he's died—an' I'm all Granny's got any more, an' I dreamed I found some money in the gutter to buy her one of them lilies, and, it's never comed true; an' I was sure it would,—an—an I'd sure like ta sell my curls to buy her one of them there lilies."

A tear fell from her shabby red coat front. The young man who was waiting was on his feet now. He took a step toward her but she did not see him. She was looking earnestly into the face of the barber in the stiff white coat.

"It's all I've got sir, an' I must sell something quick—an' my curls is all I have, an' I must hurry back to the Flower Shop, cause they are almost all gone, an I counted an' there are only eight left in the window, an' tomorrow's Granny's birthday and all, an sir, it would make her so happy, cause she cries nearly every day, an—" she stopped to catch her breath.

"Well," is all the barber said, still holding his scissors.

"How much do the flowers cost?" he asked at length.

"I don't know sir, but could you please give me a quarter for my curls? If my dream don't come true, I must some how buy me some money." The barber smiled with compassion.

"Does your grandma know you want to sell your hair?"

"Oh, no sir!" It's to be a surprise. You'll buy it, won't you, please?" Another big tear fell on her coat. Then two tears fell.

The barber took 3 pretty bouncy curls in his hand and held his scissors close.

"Don't your dare cut that little girls hair!" The young man sprang forward, placing his firm hand on the barbers arm.

"That would be a dirty shame to cut off those pretty curls. Come with me."

He took Sally Ann by the hand and together they went out of the barber shop hand in hand and went down the street directly and didn't stop until they came to the front of the Flower Shop.

"Now, little girl, you point to the flower that you want for your Granny." Sally caught her breath.

"Yes, you go ahead. You can pick out the flower that you want for your Grandma, and I'll buy it for you. Sally Ann caught her breath. She clasped her hand to her breast.

"Really sir? Is this a dream?"

"No, child, this is real." The clerk came forward. This is all we have left, sir. Most of them have all been sold. It is late, you know. The one beside you there is two dollars and fifty cents and the others are two dollars."

"I'll take this one." The young man chose the one beside him. Sally Ann and the clerk wrapped the potted lily together.

"You tell me where you live, and I will carry it home to your Grandma for you."

Sally Ann led the way. Not a word was spoken by either one in the short distance they walked to the basement door.

"Granny, open the door!" The white haired woman answered Sally Ann's call.

"It's a lily plant for your birthday Granny!" Sally Ann's face shone with an enormous smile.

"But, Sally Ann—"

"It's alright Ma'am spoke the kind man as he tipped his hat. Just a little gift, given to you in the name of our Risen Lord." He presented her with the flower package. "I couldn't bear to see her sell her—"

"Sh!" Sally Ann shook her curly head. The man turned to go.

"Oh, I want to know your name before you leave." Asked Granny, while the man stroked the child's head with all her bouncy curls, as he looked down into her happy face.

"Sally Ann." She looked up at him. "Sally Ann what?"

"Galesburg."

"Galesburg? Yes, she smiled."

"I used to work beside a Homer Galesburg at the factory here in town. Could he have been—?"

"Yes, he was my son." Granny spoke tenderly.

"And, my daddy," said Sally Ann at the same time.

"Was he really?" My name is Bond, John Bond. I am very sorry to hear of his sudden death. I was trying my best to share the wonderful things about Jesus Christ. He showed some interest in what he was being told. That very morning he took some tracts to read and promised me he would read them. I—I—"

Granny Galesburg swayed for a moment with a sickness in her soul and a longing she felt deep inside her heart.

When she tried to speak her voice died in her throat. At last she walked over to the suit on the wall, setting the lily tenderly on the table and drew from his pocket, three papers.

"These?" She had trembled and her voice was sad with emotion.

"I think so, ma'am. Homer was a fine son." Hot tears ran down Granny's cheeks.

"I—I—" she sobbed. "I can't read sir, an, I wish I knew."

"Wish you knew what?"

"Wish I knew about the future. It's all so dark to me. Homer—Homer—he," she could say no more.

"You can, Mrs. Galesburg." John Bond took a step toward her. "I'm sure you can know." His voice was confident and kind.

"Oh, Granny," Sally Ann's face beamed with new hope. "Maybe he can tell us 'bout Jesus and stuff."

"Maybe so, Honey Pet." Granny Galesburg smiled through her tears and she folded Sally Ann in her arms, and together for the first time they listened to the amazing Easter Story.

Jennie's Book

By Christmas Carol Kauffman, age 39, Hannibal, Missouri
Originally published May 4 and 11, 1941
In the Youth's Christian Companion

Jennie walked on. If she heard Mike speak, she never let him know it. A robin on the fence looked at her, chirped pleasantly, and flew away.

Hey, Jennie," Mike was nearly beside her now. His black wavy hair shone like patent leather in the hot afternoon sun. Jennie turned and looked at him in spite of herself. Mike smiled and showed two rows of splendid white teeth, and his black eyes sparkled happily.

"Let-a me carry your book-a, Mess Jennie, please-a." Mike put out his hand, but Jennie held her book tighter under her arm.

She looked at the boy without smiling. She hesitated a moment. The other children were all down the road a quarter of a mile already.

"Did-a you stay-a in, Mess Jennie, because-a Mess Brown make-a you?"

This time Jennie had to answer. She wouldn't want Mike, or Goldie, or Edith, or anyone to think she had to stay after school when she didn't.

"I stayed to help Miss Brown clean all the blackboards," answered Jennie giving her head a faint jerk, "because I like to- and not because I had to. Didn't you have to though?"

"She ask-a me to," he answered quietly, never taking his eyes from her, "for-a, me-a da lesson tomorrow. I can-a not get all the English, Mess Jennie, but-a I try-a the best'a." Mike smiled again and a dimple appeared in each fat cheek.

"Let-a me carry your book-a and your dinner box-a. My Fada, he teach-a me to be nice-a to-a the ladies."

And without another word Jennie let Mike take her book and dinner box. Together they started down the road toward Pumpkin Center, —Mike with a pink and black dinner box in one hand, and two books under his arm. The dust hung in little gray clouds behind their feet.

"You live-a in these-a village for much-a years? he asked gently, as they walked along. "Ever since my grandfather died. We came to live with my grandma then. Where did you come from?" Jennie looked straight ahead, and twisted the end of her long yellow braid and twisted her finger.

"My fader work-a in Los Angeles till he got a call-a to work-a da oil drill-a out here. He get-a a more pay-a next week-a."

"Are you the oldest in your family? Are there other children?"

"Yes-a Mess Jennie. There is Leta, an Toni, an Leo, an baby Marie-a, who don't walk-a yet. An' is she ever sweet-a! Mess Jennie, you got-a see her once to know how-a sweet-a she is-a, but Scampy, he's da pumpkins man at the Pumpkin Center, Fada says."

Jennie Owens chuckled, real, real softly. Her cheeks got pink.

"Cause-a he always does-a such cute things, and with-a no try-a. He's so small-a for his size-a and so smart-a. Some day-a if Mess Brown-a don care-a, I'll bring-a him to school-a. "Have you-a no brothers or sisters-a, Miss Jennie?" He looked straight at her.

"I have two sisters but they're married. And I have one cute little brother, James. He's almost old enough to start school."

Jennie twisted her braid again. They biked on in silence until they reached the crossroad.

To the north about three rods stood a two-story brick house, well kept for its age. A big shepherd dog ran to the edge of the velvety grass and looked down the road, past the rose bushes and came bounding toward Jennie. Around and around her he went, at the same time barking at the pink dinner box Mike held with his own black one.

"What-a you want-a?" asked Mike, holding the dinner box above his head. The dog jumped up. Hadn't he seen the dog bound down that same road every evening at four when Jennie reached the corner? Hadn't he seen her put her pink dinner box in his mouth, and then walk down the road while the dog ran ahead of her? Hadn't he followed Jennie Owens and Patsy Ann Fieldhouse from school to the crossroads for over three weeks now? Of course he did not walk on their heels, but a gentlemanly distance behind. Hadn't he often heard Jennie's voice ring out in laughter as the two girls jabbered in school-girl fashion as they walked? Mike liked the way Jennie laughed. He liked the way Jennie walked. He liked her dainty feet, and her long blond hair. Why he even liked her pink dinner box for some reason or other. But tonight—this was the first time that Patsy Ann had gone on with the other girls. Mike was really almost glad. He—he was glad. His black eyes glowed with radiant joy. He actually walked beside Jennie tonight, not behind her, and carried her dinner box and arithmetic book!

"He wants my dinner box, Mike. He likes it and wants to take it home for me; then I give him what's left Brownie, you will get one crust tonight," and Jennie patted the dog fondly, "only one, and a half ginger snap. And there's a dill pickle in there too, but you don't like them," she laughed.

"Here-a you are, Brownie. Fine-a dog-a you are to-a carry Mess Jennie's dinner box." Mike lowered the pink box, and Brownie took the handles between his teeth. He looked at Jennie as if to ask, "Are you going now?"

"Bye," said Jennie shyly as she took her book from Mike.

"Good-by-a, Mess Jennie," returned Mike, looking her straight in the face. "Come over sometime-a and see Marie-a and Scampy."

"Which house is yours?"

"Well, you see-a that one-a with the new chimney, and a little red-a wagon? That's-a where I live-a, Mess Jennie."

"I see. Come on, Brownie; let's go, but don't kick up so much dust. You get me so dirty."

Jennie and Patsy Ann walked home together every night the next week, and the next, and Mike with a group of boys.

One rainy day Miss Brown asked the children to play inside during the noon hour.

"I'll let the sixth graders choose games today," announced the teacher after they had all finished their lunches. "Mary, have you a game to suggest?"

Mary scratched her head, and bit her fingers. Mary never could think on such occasions. Several hands went up, and fingers snapped.

"Teacher, teacher, I know—I know."

"Sh. Hands down. I'm thinking of a number between ten and twenty."

"Eleven—fourteen—seventeen—twelve—nineteen."

"Nineteen is right," announced the teacher. "Jennie, what shall we play?"

"Trains Are Passing." Answered Jennie.

"Good!" shouted the children, and without delay they formed a circle in the front of the room. But, Mike kept his seat.

"Don't you want to play, Mike?"

Mike shook his head.

"Why not?" asked Miss Brown.

"I know-a not how-a, Mess Brown," came the answer.

Mike blushed. Somehow he shrunk from being the object of laughter too often. Every day the girls tittered and the boys snickered at something he had said in Italian accent. And now it was another new game to learn! Again he shook his head.

"I listen this time-a, please, Mess Brown." He leaned his head on his one hand.

"Come on-a, Mike-a," blurted out big Oscar, who took delight in mimicking this new pupil. "I'll call-a the town's-a—"

"Oscar," Miss Brown's hand was on his fat arm, "you could speak English a little better yourself for a boy your age and size."

Oscar scowled angrily and muttered something under his breath as he took his seat. He made a face at Mike when the teacher turned her back.

After the children had played "Trains Are Passing" for ten minutes, the teacher said, "Now Mike, don't you think you could play the game?"

"I know-a so little a city, Mess Brown." Oscar clapped one hand over his mouth, but the suppressed laughter squirted out between his fingers.

"Oscar," spoke Miss Brown, "if that happens again, I'll keep you after school." And he knew she meant it. Oscar laid his head on his arms and pretended to go to sleep.

The game continued. New York train passed Buffalo, and Kansas City passed Wichita, and Pumpkin Ville crashed into the Chicago train. Herman got a lump on his forehead, and little Nina lost her loose tooth. A few tears were shed, and the game was changed.

"What shall we play now, Helen?"

"Under the Tub."

"You know how to play that, Mike?" She came close. She leaned toward him.

"Not-a so very much."

"Are you sick, Mike?"

He shook his head.

"Are you worried?"

"Ah, not-a much, Mess Brown."

The afternoon dragged on. Most of the children were wiry and dull in recitations. Even Bonnie who never had acted bad, had to be called down for whispering, and Edith missed two spelling words. Mike's face was flushed and his eyes burned. The rain fell in a steady drizzle, and by four o'clock it was half dark.

"Well, children," spoke the teacher in a tired voice. "I hate to send you home in this rain. But I do hope you'll all go to bed early and get a good night's rest, and be feeling better tomorrow. You are dismissed!"

Jennie's father was waiting in a car outside. Some fathers can do that on rainy days.

"Come, Patsy Ann; Daddy is here to take us home." They scrambled into the front seat.

"Hello, girls. How are you? We might as well take a load. Davy—Carl, jump in; you might as well have a ride too. And the new boy. He lives down our way, too, doesn't he, Jennie?"

"Mike" Yes."

"Mike," called Mr. Owens, "ride along? It won't cost you anything this time. Jump in."

"How was school today?" asked Mr. Owens, as they started down the road. Davy looked at Carl and Carl looked at Mike.

"Don't all speak at once," he laughed. "Did you all stand in the corner?"

"No one of us did." Answered Jennie.

"Well, when I was a boy the teacher said we always acted up bad on rainy days." The children grinned. All but Mike. Davy, Carl and Patsy Ann got out at the crossroads.

"Stay in. Mike; I'll drive you home. I have a little business down your way, anyhow." The house with the new chimney was the next to the last one in the row.

As the car stopped to let Mike out, Mr. Owens thought (he was not sure) that he saw a woman standing inside the doorway, crying.

"Father,"Jennie looked straight ahead as they drove farther down the road..........Father, do you know I think Mike is—well anyway, its not a bit nice how some of the pupils make fun of the way he talks."

"And you never have?" He looked down at her.

"Why, Father! Of course not."

***

Mike's seat was empty the next day, and the next; and the third day Miss Brown asked Jennie to stay after school and help her clean the blackboards.

"And you like to, Jennie?"

"Oh, of course I do, Miss Brown."

"Jennie." she said at length. "Do you know why Mike has been absent?"

"No I don't, Miss Brown."

"Do you know where he lives?"

"Yes, I do."

"It's down your way isn't it?"

"Yes."

"Then we'll walk together." Jennie smiled. At the crossroads Jennie pointed out the house.

"Do you see which one I mean, Miss Brown?"

"Yes, but why not walk along?"

"I guess I can."

"Oh, isn't this breeze lovely?"

They threw back their heads, and walked in the glory of it. The day had been hot, as some days are in September.

"What is that, Miss Brown?" Jennie pointed toward the next to the last house. Miss Brown noticed it too. Together they took a few more steps.

"Scarlet fever? Jennie!"

A short, heavy set woman stood in the open doorway. She held a little girl in her arms. She looked frightened.

"Mrs. Feiglio?" Spoke Miss Brown.

"Yes."

"I am Mike's school teacher." Does he have scarlet fever?"

"Yes."

"Is he very sick, Mrs. Feigilo?"

"Yes." Her eyes glistened with tears.

"Does the baby have it too?"

"Not-a yet-a." Her lips trembled.

"Is there anything we can do for you, Mrs? Feiglio?" She did not answer.

"I'd be glad to do something for you, or for Mike, if there is anything I can do. Tell me." Still the woman did not answer.

"I no speak-much English," she said at length.

"My Mike-a, he very sick-a. My Leo—my Tony, very sick-a. My Marie-a," and at this, the woman broke out in sobs as she held her baby close to her. Miss Brown and Jennie both found tears in their eyes too.

"You have a good doctor, I suppose?"

"Doctor—doctor—but no priest-a near. My Mike-a so sick-a."

Miss Brown stepped a little closer then, as close as she felt she dared. The red sign beside the door was not there for nothing.

"Is Mike by the window? Could I see him? Mrs. Feiglio?"

She pointed toward the next room. The bed was not close to a window, and anyway, the blind was drawn.

"Well, Mrs. Feiglio, I'll pray for Mike and his brothers and sister. I am so sorry that I did not come sooner. I noticed last Monday in school that Mike was not feeling very well. I haven't heard of any other cases of scarlet fever, but I will surely pray for your children. Tell Mike we called. Tell him and your other children that we will be praying for them, won't we, Jennie?"

"Yes, Mrs. Feiglio, I'll pray too. God can do more than a priest." The woman looked dumbfounded.

"Do the children have what they need to eat?" asked the teacher.

She shook her head slowly. "Mike's Fada work-a da oil drill-a. He quit-a to help-a. He go-a to town-a for orange an' ice-a."

Late that evening Mike sat up in bed, with a strange look on his face. He held out one hand.

"Jennie," he called feebly, "Jennie, come closer."

"Mike!" His father stood by the bed.

"Give it to me-a Jennie." Mike still held out one hand. "Give it to me-a. Oh, Jennie."

"Mike, don't!" His father put his arm around him. "Who is Jennie?"

"There she is-a Fada. Don't-a you see her beautiful dress-a?"

"Poor Mike, lay-a down. Poor Mike. Let me get-a more ice on your head-a. You know not-a you speak-a." There was a knock at the door.

"Mr. Feiglio?" Spoke a kind voice outside. "I am Mr. Owens. My daughter Jennie came home this evening and told me you folks here had scarlet fever."

"Yes, sir."

"And I brought some oranges for your children; and I have fifty pounds of ice out in my car for you, too. I had scarlet fever once when I was a boy, and I remember yet, how horrible I felt."

"Very kind of you, Meester."

"Are your children very sick?"

"Mike is very sick-a, Meester. He talk-a like he see Jennie an' no Jennie there-a."

"Well, here is a little book Jennie sent over for him. Little words of comfort from the Word of God. She marked one verse on page 28. Tell him to be sure to read it. All the verses are good, Mr. Feiglio. Read them to Mike, if he can't read. I suppose you can read English?"

"Some-a, Yes-a. But-a this book-a, you say?"

"It is some precious promises out of the Word of God, Mr. Feiglio. Every word is true. The verse Jennie has marked reads like this: 'What things so ever ye desire when ye pray, believe that ye shall receive them, and ye shall have them."

"But, no priest lives here, Meester."

"Oh, sir, but God is here by you. He hears when me and you pray. We need no priest. He hears and answers our prayers, both yours and mine. Just believe in Him. Tell Mike to—"

"Fada, Fada," called Mike.

"Good night, Mr. Feiglio, I'll come back in the morning."

"Thank you Meester, come back in the morn-a."

"Fada, Jennie's book-a." He handed Mike the small brown book. Feebly the boy clasped it to his heart and sank back on his pillow.

"It was Jennie's Fada, Mike, who brought-a da book-a."

"Jennie did," he insisted. The man stroked Mike's head. "Let me read-a the verse-a she mark-a for you-a. Poor Mike."

Slowly, Mr. Feiglio read with some difficulty the underscored verse. Jennie had it marked with red crayon. "Read it again-a Fada." He did. "Once more-a Fada." And he did.

"When ye pray-a? Oh, Fada, I know-a not how-a. Can you tell-a me how-a?"

The man looked bewildered. His wife was hovering over Leo in the adjoining room. Tony was crying for a drink. And now Mike was asking for something harder to give than a drink; harder to give than orange juice.

"Miss Brown-a she pray-a in school-a, Fada, like that-a you think-a?"

"Ah, Mike, my boy, I guess-a. Oh, Mike, I wish-awe knew-a." The man fell on his knees beside the bed clasping the little brown book in both hands.

Just below that verse he read this one. "If ye shall ask anything in my name, I will do it." On he read: "The Son of man is come to seek and to save that which was lost. Whosoever believeth in Him shall receive re-remission of sins."

"Oh, Mike, this is a very strange book-a. I—I—" He shook his head slowly.

"It must be a good book-a Fada. Read Jennie's verse again." Again, he read slowly, those comforting and precious words. Mike's lips began to move. His father listened intently, but could not understand.

"Tomorrow morning I talk-a more da man to bring-a this book-a", he whispered to himself.

"Mike, Mike, are you going to sleep? Mike, Mike," He touched him. He bent over him. "Mike." Mike smiled faintly.

"Jennie's book-a shine like a lamp-a. Fada, I—I follow da book-a. See—See— Fada?"

***

"How's Mike this morning, Mr Feiglio?" Mr. Owens was at the door. He did not need to knock, for Mike's father saw him coming.

"Oh, Meester," the man sobbed broken. Oh, Meester, Mike—my Mike is dead-a!"

"What?" Mr. Owens caught his breath. He caught the porch post for support. "The day light-a, oh Meester, Mike ask-a for da book-a. He hold it so close-a, an' say-a "Nice book-a—Jennie—good book-a, Jennie—it shine-a da way-a for me-a. Oh, Meester!" The man shook with great sobs. "I must know 'bout that book-a too. It make-a Mike so happy, he smile, but my heart-a— Oh, Meester, is broke-a."

"But the Book sir, will heal it. I promise I will teach you more, and what it teaches us is true, for ever and for sure!"

Never Alone

By Christmas Carol Kauffman, age 34, Hannibal Missouri
Originally published March 14 and 21, 1937
in the Youth's Christian Companion

It was shortly past midnight. All was quiet in the dingy little house. A mouse ventured halfway across the room and ran back.

Evelyn had not been asleep long. Sleep was something she had to beg God to send her these nights; these long, anxious terrible nights when mother went off in a fit of anger, and said she'd be back when she got ready. Yes; when Steve Smith got ready to bring her back, staggering, stumbling to the door, and shove her inside. It used to be John Hayse, and before that, Joe Norris, and Evelyn well remembered when a man by the name of Charlie used to come in their home over on Harvy Aveue, and her mother would wrap her in a blanket and take her over to an old lady, and tell her to behave herself and she'd come and get her in the morning. Often it was nearly noon before she came, and the old lady would beg and plead with Mable to quit her running around with wicked men, and be a real mother to dear little Evelyn. Mable always half promised.

"There; there; Evelyn, honey," the old lady would say as she took the child up in her arms. "God bless and keep this little child, and make her grow up to be a good, decent Christian woman and never turn out to be like her mother. God love her; God love her tiny heart. Sit here on my lap by the fire, honey, and I'll tell ye a pretty story' 'til your blue eyes go shut, shut, shut. Then I'll put you in the bed right side o' me 'til mornin'."

That was at least twelve years ago, and since then Mable and Evelyn had moved from there to here, and from here to there a dozen times or more, and tonight Evelyn found herself alone again in a crooked tumble-down shack off the end of Chase Street, alone and after midnight, alone with her troubles and never-ceasing heartaches—crushing, piercing, smothering heartaches.

Steve had called at seven o'clock, and Mable left, giving Evelyn strict orders to wash up all the dirty dishes and scrub the floor before she sat down to get her arithmetic problem and when she went to bed she was to let the light burn. In no uncertain terms and with harsh accent, Steve thrust his head into the door and said, "Now mind what yer mother told you, Evy."

"Evy"—oh, how she hated to be called Evy. And who was Steve Smith to order her around, and by what right did he call so often and take her mother to—where—oh—where did they go in that old car and stay so long, and why was her mother so hateful the next day? She made no answer.

Evelyn stood at the window until the car was out of sight, but that was not long, for sudden tears blinded her eyes. She made her way to a broken chair, (that was the only kind there was in the house) buried her face in her hands, and cried as though her heart would break. Grief in thick clouds pressed in upon her, black and stifling, until she had to catch her throat and gasp for breath. Something was crushing her around the heart. She thought she would faint or maybe die, but people do not faint or die so easily as they think they can or wish they could.

There was a gentle knock outside. Evelyn jumped. She was too startled to go to the door.

"Evelyn," a sweet voice called.

Instantly the girl was on her feet.

"Come in, Miss Revell," she said softly.

No words of apology were necessary. Miss Revell had called before and understood. Nevertheless, Evelyn's hot face got hotter, and her lips trembled.

She found herself that same moment in the woman's arms.

"What's the matter, Evelyn? You're crying."

"Oh, nothing."

"But, Evelyn, something has happened. Tell me, dear."

"I can't."

"Can't you tell your Sunday-school teacher? Would I not understand?"

"I don't know." The girl was crying again now. Softly now, for the arms of Miss Revell felt kind and strong.

"Mother gone again?"

Evelyn nodded.

"And why didn't you come to church last night, Evelyn? I missed you. I thought maybe you were sick, so I came out to see."

There was no reply. Evelyn's body trembled and a hot tear fell on the teacher's hand. "Were you sick, Evelyn?" The teacher's voice was very low.

"I had a terrible headache, and the snow—"

"Yes; it was wet and bad outside. Did you go to school today?"

She nodded.

"When did your mother leave?"

"Just a little while ago." She could hardly speak. Great sobs came now uncontrolled.

"Don't, Evelyn, dear. I wish I could bear it for you. Tell me—tell me what's on your heart. You are troubled. I never saw you quite like this.

"Oh!' she cried. "Oh, my mother! The harder I try to do what's right the worse she acts. The—the more I read my Bible the more she scolds me. The more I pray the worse she curses me, and the oftener I go to church the more she makes me do here at home until I think it's—"

"What?"

"Oh, Miss Revell, I want to be a Christian. I love the church. I want to go on, but it's so hard."

"I know, dear, but doesn't it make you happy to know you are God's child?"

"Yes; I know I am, but—"

"But you don't want to give up now."

"No; but my mother is so wicked I get slurred in school. Some of the girls won't be seen on the street with me. I wish sometimes I could have died when my father did. Most of the other girls in the church have nice homes, and real mothers. I never knew what a—a real—real mother was and—and she told me last night that if she ever hears me pray for her once more she'll beat me to death."

"Really, Evelyn?" The teacher's eyes were blurred now. She took Evelyn's hand in her own. There were marks on it.

Evelyn tried to pull her hand away, but Miss Revell held it.

"Did she ever beat you?"

"Many times."

"For what?"

"For praying."

"Beat you for praying? My God! What a testimony. What little persecution I've gone through is not worth mentioning. Evelyn, there will be a crown for you some day; and still you pray?"

"I can't stop. Not if she beats me to death! She was out with Steve Saturday night and came home drunk Sunday morning. She was still sleeping when I went to Sunday school and still sleeping when I came home. I knelt down here by this chair and was praying for her, and I guess I forgot myself a little, and all at once she was standing over me with the stove poker, and—"

"And made those marks on your hand?" Miss Revell's breath came sharp and quick. Thoughts of her own dear little mother who taught her how to sing and pray, who showed her tenderly and carefully the ways of salvation accompanied the thoughts of this heartless, vile being. Evelyn's own mother! How sharp the contrast; how cruel and unfair it all seemed that Evelyn, young and beautiful, brilliant and so unusually talented, could not have had a better chance—at least half a chance!

"Well, listen, Evelyn; just listen to me, dear. Jesus was beaten for our sakes, beaten because He was doing good. Whenever you are scoffed at or ridiculed or struck at, remember that Jesus is the one who feels it. Of course it hurts you, but it hurts Him far more. He has promised that if we follow Him, we will receive persecution, and I sometimes wonder if we who are so little persecuted are really following Him as we should. If you were beaten for doing a wrong, I could not pity you,—but for praying! Oh, Evelyn, how God must love you; how sweet and blessed will be your reward. You do not feel like giving up, now; surely?"

She shook her head.

"No, not since you came. I was discouraged tonight. All these dishes, and the floor, and lessons, and I am alone so much! But I would not mind that if only mother would come to church with me and get saved."

"You don't think there's any hope?"

"I don't know. Sometimes I think maybe she stays away because of conviction, and sometimes I think she is past hope. Whenever I think of my father—"

"Then what, dear?"

"Well I want go to go on and be able to meet him someday."

"Was he a Christian?"

"Mother said he was. I never knew before, but—" Evelyn was walking the floor now, her hands clasped in front of her. A strange light shone from her big blue eyes, and in the dimness of the oil light on the shelf, there was a beauty on the girl's face her teacher could not explain. A sudden halo of beauty hovered over her, a holy heavenly expression that almost startled her. She bent forward, motionless, and watched Evelyn walk back and forth.

"'Stop it!' My mother cried," She said. "Stop that silly praying this minute before I strike you. You're just like your father, always praying for me. Save her for Jesus' sake," she mimicked. "Save her, nothin'. This salvation is all blah-blah. Don't ever let me hear you pray for me. Get up off your knees. That's the very reason why I left your father when you were two years old. I left him before you were old enough to learn that crazy foolishness. If I'd have stayed with him he'd made a Christian out of you long ago. The older you get, the more you are like him. I wish I'd never let you start goin' down there to that old Sunday school. I sent you off to get rid of you, and now see the fool you've turned out to be. A Christian—Christian indeed? Wearing one of those silly prayer caps and running to church all the time. You'll never get a man. You good-for-nothin'.' And just then; oh, Miss Revell! My mother —she—she opened that trunk there and got out an envelope, and took out a picture and held it before me; 'There's your father,' she screamed; 'take one good look at him once. You look just like him. just exactly.' Oh, Miss Revell, I never saw him before—a picture—I mean. Oh, he looked so good and kind. Oh, so—so Christian like and good. I reached for the picture, and just then she lifted the stove lid. I tried to get it. I screamed and begged and cried, but it's gone! She stuck it in the fire. It's gone! My father! My father! I want him so. She was half drunk, and I don't know if she realizes she told me. I am afraid to bring it up. She is so unreasonable. I can't talk to her. Oh, Miss Revell!" and the girl threw her arms around her Sunday school teacher. "If it weren't for you and the dear people in the church, what would I do and where would I be tonight? And—and, I wonder if my father is in heaven praying for me, or is he still alive somewhere? I wish I knew."

"Is he not dead, Evelyn?"

"I don't know. I thought so until yesterday. She said she wished she could put me in a box and ship me to him. I asked her if he didn't die when I was two years old, and she just laughed and said she didn't know. She always told me he died, but yesterday she said he was praying the last time she saw him. If I only knew!"

"Is there no way of finding out?" It was the teacher now who was pacing the floor. She bit her lips and coughed, nervously.

"Evelyn," her voice was husky and strange.

Evelyn jumped.

"Where did you live when your mother left your father?"

"She never told me."

"What was the real reason why she left him? Do you know, dear?"

I told you all I know. Every time I asked about him, she told me to keep still and not mention the dead."

"But your relatives—who are they and where do they live?"

"I don't know. I am absolutely alone in this world. Sometimes I even wonder if my mother is my mother. All I am sure of is that Jesus is mine and I am His."

"Well, praise God for that, Evelyn. That's worth more than all earthly ties we can claim. Oh, you precious child; thank God for the day you came walking into my Sunday school class last June. And I'm going to do these dishes and the floor while you get your lessons."

"Oh, never! Miss Revell. These dirty dishes—never!"

"Yes!" Now when Miss Revell said "yes" in that way, Evelyn knew better than to contradict.

So the dishes were washed and stacked and the floor scrubbed while Evelyn worked her problems, and not a word was spoken by either until nine o'clock.

"Now we're going to read a chapter, sing a song, and pray before you go to bed. I hate to leave you before your mother comes back, but it probably would be best."

"Yes, it would be best."

"I don't suppose your mother would love me for coming here like this."

"No, but I do." Evelyn smiled the first smile that evening.

Softly and lovingly Miss Revell read verses from the fourteenth and seventeenth chapters of St. John's Gospel, and together they sang that blessed song, "No, Never Alone." At first Evelyn could not help.

There was no music in her throat tonight, but before she knew it, unconsciously she was singing, too.

"I have a friend so precious;

So very dear to me.

He loves me with such tender love—

Loves me so faithfully.

I could not live apart from Him.

I long to feel Him nigh;

And so we dwell together—

My precious Lord and I."

Evelyn smiled, and her eyes were toward heaven.

"No, never alone; no, never alone; He promised never to leave me. Never to leave me alone."

***

Together they knelt beside the bed, and such a prayer as Evelyn poured out to God few have ever heard. With renewed determination and courage to keep on, and be true to God no matter what the future held in store for her, she got to her feet, kissed her teacher good night, and got ready for bed. The trunk stood in the corner of the room beyond the bed. Evelyn brought the light closer and lifted the lid. Her fingers trembled as she removed one at a time the garments and laid them on the bed. She looked out the window but saw nothing but the houses across the street. It was 10:30, and it was 10:45 when Evelyn put everything back into the trunk just as she found it. Life was full of disappointments; mysteries and broken bubbles; dreams that never came true.

It was shortly past midnight and Evelyn had just fallen asleep. Ten blocks away Miss Revell sat at her desk in deep, troubled thought. Before her lay an open album and a letter which she had received that day.

Dear Helen:

How are you enjoying your work—especially the church work? God has given me strength such as I never knew, especially since my ordination, but no one knows my loneliness, especially at times. Pray for me. I may see you in a few weeks.

Sincerely, your brother, Lloyd

She caught up her pen and wrote just a line on a card.

Dear Lloyd:

By all means stop to see me, and will I ever be glad!

Love,

Helen

And then followed a sealed letter to another part of the state.

Dear Mother and Father:

Lloyd writes he may see me in a few weeks. If Schlink's take their trip to New York, I can come home for awhile; and maybe Lloyd and I can come together. I am well and enjoy my work, especially the class in Sunday school. I still get all day Sunday off. Please send me that picture of Lloyd and little Eleanor soon and that clipping from the Pittsburgh paper. How are you? God bless and keep you.

Love, Helen

Evelyn was in her usual place in church the next evening—a sad yet peaceful look of mingled wonder and hope was written there. When she got home her mother was huddled close to the stove a ————-- ———— magazine in her hand,

"Mother!" Evelyn stood close to her mother.

"Don't tell me about reading these magazines, little Christian," she snapped.

"No; mother, although I couldn't read them myself. What was my father's name?"

"Your father's name?" Her eyes became slits and she threw the magazine to the floor. "What do you suppose his name was?"

"His first name, mother. You never told me that, and I'd love to know."

"You are better off not to know that, young lady, and don't get smart around here, now. Who has been stuffin' you, anyway?"

"No one has been stuffing me, but I can't help but wonder about some things.

"Neither can I."

Evelyn washed out several pieces of clothing for herself, read her Bible, knelt beside her bed a few minutes in silent prayer and went to bed.

The woman across the room kept her eyes on the magazine but turned no pages. An hour she sat there thus. Slowly, she crept over to the bed and listened; yes; Evelyn was asleep. She tiptoed to the trunk and took everything out carefully; she lifted from the bottom an old and faded newspaper that lined the trunk. A fitful dream made Evelyn open her eyes wide. Crossing the room the woman laid the paper on the table and bent over it. Evelyn could hear her breathe heavily and give a loud sigh. She had never heard her mother sigh like that before. She wilted across the table and her head fell with a thud on the newspaper. Her body shook and shook; Evelyn caught her breath. Her heart thumped until she could hear it. Her mother might hear it! The woman folded the paper in a tight wad, stuck it behind the clock, and blew out the light. Long after that she came to bed, but neither mother nor daughter slept until morning.

The next evening Steve called again for Mable. An hour later, Evelyn closed her school books and slipped her hand behind the clock. The paper was gone! Disappointment again! Or would it have been a greater disappointment to know what it all meant? Why had she not noticed the newspaper the night she emptied the trunk? Just an old, faded newspaper. But what did it tell? Evelyn looked through all the drawers, searched every conceivable place where she thought the paper might be tucked away, but her search was fruitless.

"Perhaps in the stove," she whispered to herself in despair. "It may have meant nothing, anyway."

One week passed. Seven days chock-full of trials for Evelyn. Ridicule and scoffings; scoldings and taunts almost unbearable! Constant words of encouragement and sympathy from Miss Revell helped keep her on the side of victory in Christ Jesus. Without a doubt there were many tears until Evelyn's young face was beginning to look old already. Her step was not so light; as usual she was reserved and quiet. The other girls all noticed it, but no one except her teacher understood the struggles in her fourteen-year-old heart.

The letter Helen Revell was anxiously looking for came. The picture of Lloyd and little Eleanor and the clipping from the Pittsburgh paper, dated June 3, 1925.

Dear Helen: (her mother wrote)

What do you want with this picture and clipping? Do not destroy them. We will be so glad to have you and Lloyd home again if only this could be cleared up once and set my old heart at rest before I pass over Jordan's stormy bank. This is the cross of my life. I cannot get over it. I have asked God many times why this trial had to come to us, and I am at as great a loss now as at first. I am happy to know God is using Lloyd, but what a mighty instrument in God's hands he might be if things were as we had all longed for them to be. Father is growing old fast. Is it any wonder? Bring home all the cheer you can.

Your loving Mother

Helen Revell ran downstairs to answer the telephone.

"Can you come out right away?"

"Evelyn?"

"Yes."

"Trouble?"

"Yes."

"I'll come if Mrs. Schlink will let me off. Yes; she said I could. I'll be there right away."

"Lloyd," she turned to her brother. Take a chair here by the fireplace. I'm sorry I have to leave as soon as you got here, but one of my girls is in trouble and called. I ought to go."

"Well, let me take you out. Just tell me the way."

"But you're tired and cold. I can catch the bus."

"Come on," and he took her by the arm.

"This is a pitiful case, Lloyd. I don't know when I've ever met up with anything so heart-rending and pitiful. A young girl trying to live a Christian life and her mother abuses her constantly."

"Why?"

"I think because she is living in such condemnation, and you know how the devil uses people who have a guilty conscience."

"Yes, indeed. And her father?"

"That's the mystery. She thought her father was dead until a week ago Sunday. While her mother was partly drunk, she said things and intimated that he might still be living. She beat her with a poker for praying for her and said that's why she ran off from her husband long ago."

"What?" Lloyd's hands grew limp on the steering wheel. "How long ago?"

"When Evelyn was two."

"Evelyn?"

"This is the place, Lloyd."

"I'll wait here."

Evelyn met Miss Revell at the door. Her face was ghastly white, and she stared wildly, like a lost child. At the same moment she heard moans—most pitiful moans—and saw a woman lying face downward on the bed.

"My mother," the girl sobbed. "When I got home from school, Steve Smith just drove away. Never spoke a word. He had been drinking—I could tell."

They stood over the woman. "I never saw your mother before. Why, Evelyn, how thin and old she looks. You said she is only thirty-three?"

Evelyn nodded.

"Her name?"

"Mable."

"Mable—Mable." Miss Revell touched her gently. No answer, only moans.

"Let's try to turn her over, Evelyn." There was a spot of blood on the bed and an ugly wound on the side of her head.

"Have you called a doctor, dear?"

"No."

Helen ran to the car and told Lloyd to phone Dr. Dans—413.

"Don't cry, Evelyn. The doctor will be here soon. She may only be stunned. Let's prop her head up higher. Get a wet towel. Yes. Now let's put that comforter here under her head. Wait; let's just lift up the mattress and put it below so it won't get bloody; see."

Together they lifted the mattress and there—there was that folded, faded newspaper. Evelyn caught it quickly and turned away.

"What is it, dear?"

"I don't know , yet. Ssh."

The woman muttered something. They both bent low.

"What is it, mother?"

"Evelyn—Evelyn," her voice was thick and unnatural.

"Yes; mother."

"Try to find your—your father; and go to him. I'm done —for."

"But how can I, mother?" Evelyn clutched at her. "Where? How?"

"Look in the—no; behind. Look—look under the mattress. Lloyd—Lloyd Murphy—Lloyd," she mumbled, half crying.

"What?" It was Miss Revell who turned white, now; and trembled from head to foot.

"Let me see that paper, Evelyn." She unfolded it and there on the front page of the Pittsburgh Daily Post, June 3, 1925, in small type she pointed it out, and Evelyn read:

MOTHER AND CHILD DISAPPEAR

Mrs. Maggie Murphy, 21 year-old wife of Lloyd Murphy, 201 Thornburn St. and 2 year-old Eleanor June disappeared from their home some time yesterday between two and four o'clock. Mrs. Murphy was last seen at the Senson Grocery near the Murphy residency. Mr. Murphy told officers that at 5:30 p.m. he received a mysterious phone call from a man who said he was given instructions to inform him that he was not to worry or search; that his wife and child had left this part of the country to live with someone who could show her a good time. Lloyd Murphy is known to all of his neighbors as a man of extraordinary character and high ideals; he is employed at the Standard Printing Co., and has been attending night school in preparation for entering the ministry. Mr. Murphy suffered a slight heart attack last evening. His condition was not serious this morning, it was reported.

While Evelyn read, her teacher stared first at the girl then at the woman—the girl whose face spoke of godly things, and the woman whose face was wretched with sin. How could it be? How dare it be?

"Lloyd?" He was at the door now. "Is the doctor coming?"

He nodded.

The woman opened her eyes and gave a frightful outcry.

"What!" He stepped closer and stopped.

"Lloyd," again the woman made a fearful outcry.

"Maggie—My God!" He fell on his knees beside the bed. He noticed another figure beside him. "Is this Eleanor?"

"Yes," the woman whispered faintly.

"My baby. My own, little Eleanor! Am I dreaming, or—or—"

"I got my--my just dues, Lloyd, today. I left you alone —no reason for it. Sin—sin—sin! My wages is death. John promised big things if I'd leave you. He's dead and gone—I was ashamed to come back, then; so on I went deeper in sin, black sin. Oh! —Steve tried to kill me today—I'm done. Take Evelyn—Eleanor—teach her; I see it now—too late—forgive—" She muttered more, but no one could understand.

The doctor! What? No hope at all? Call an ambulance.

Lloyd Murphy's great father-heart reached out, and the girl's long-broken, troubled heart reached out, and together their arms clasped around each other. They wept both for sorrow and for joy. He kissed her face and hair.

Before the ambulance arrived, the soul of the woman departed from the body never to return.

"Oh, Eleanor! My child! How you've changed. Can it be—at last. How lonely I've been!"

"And how lonely I've been," she sobbed on his shoulder.

"Call me 'Father,' just once, darling."

Her big blue eyes searched his through and through.

"Father," she whispered.

"You'll never be lonely again for me, dear."

"Never lonely again? Oh, Father." She touched his cheek with her hand. "Never alone, and you'll keep me with you always?"

"Always, dear; as long as we both shall live."

"'I have a friend so precious'—Know it? It has helped me through many a lonely night."

"No; never alone, Eleanor, my child—never—never!" He pointed toward the skies.

Her Mother's Son

By Christmas Carol Kauffman, age 26, Hannibal Missouri
Originally published February 10, 17, and 24, 1929
in the Youth's Christian Companion

A tear trickled gently down the face of the girl as she was setting the kitchen table for two. She took the corner of her blue gingham apron and wiped it away, but when her glance met that ever-understanding, ever-anxious one from the eyes of her mother's picture on the clock shelf, the girl leaned hard against the wall and cried out in pitiful broken sobs.

"Oh mother—mother dear!" The girl clasped the picture to her breast. "For your sake I'll never give up. God will answer our prayers someday—someday, mother. I'll die praying for Matt. He can't ever forget you, mother—no."

The sleet outside was beginning to turn into beautiful fluffy flakes. Before long the earth, the shrubbery and every catchable thing was covered with a blanket of white. Men and women were hurrying home from their places of business, news boys were calling out the evening paper, and the bell in the St. Monica's Church steeple rang for six o'clock prayer.

In the kitchen of the scantily furnished three-room apartment stood Emily Dune preparing the supper on a little oil stove. She always fixed things that were easily kept and warmed over, because she never knew when Matt would be home.

Since mother died Matt had gone from bad to worse, and Emily's heart had grown from sadness to the utter depression of grief. Matt was twenty when their mother had her last heart attack. Emily was alone with her when it happened, and her last whispering words were, "Emily, br—bring Matt."

"I will, mother," sobbed Emily, "but don't leave us—I will—mother speak—my God, my God!"

Half an hour later Matt came stumbling in half drunk, his clothes wet and his shoes sopping.

"Oh, Matt, why didn't you come straight home tonight just for once. Matt, mother is—is dead."

That experience made an impression on Matt which lasted only two weeks. After selling most of the household goods to pay the funeral expenses the two orphans moved into the three-room apartment and every night when Emily came home from the printing office, she built the fire, prepared the meal, and waited, waited. It was the same experience tonight.

The girl bathed her face at the sink and smoothed back her auburn hair. She sat by the window for some time and watched the long purple shadows deepening into black. Crossing the room she took from the clock shelf a small worn Bible of her mother's. It opened up at a page where a pressed red rose had been placed, and her eyes fell on a verse that had been underlined with red. "The eternal God is thy refuge and underneath are the everlasting arms." A faint smile lit up her wan, troubled face, and lifting it toward heaven she prayed.,

"Eternal God, I rest my soul in your—"

The door burst open and Matt covered with heavy wet snow, sank, without removing cap or coat, into the nearest chair.

"Well is the grub ready to eat, kid?" He bawled out in guttural, drunken glib.

"Yes, Matt—I—but—come over by the stove, Matt. You'll catch your death of cold."

"Cold, nothin'. Got hot coffee? The boys are comin' 'long at eight o'clock, an' what time is it now, sis? I can't see that—eh—this light is do dim."

"Matt, the light is all right. It's your eyes—you've been drinking again. It's ten minutes till—"

"Ten minutes till eight?" He fairly yelled the words at her. "Get the stuff on the table hot or cold!"

"Yes, Matt, it will be ready as soon as you are washed."

He rose to go to the sink, staggered and caught his balance by the open cupboard door.

"I'd rather you stay in tonight, Matt," Her voice was pensive and wistful. "I want to talk to you, Matt."

She placed the potatoes and meat on the table wearily.

"Don't start in like that again, Sis," he growled. "I know what you're up to again. Some more of that Church stuff —baby talk—mush—mother's little boy. I'm sick of it!"

His eyes glared wildly and his fists clenched tightly. He came close to Emily, till she could feel his hot insulting breath in her pale, frightened face. He had never spoken like this to her before. A strange fear seized her.

"If you ever say another word to me about my affairs, Emily Dune, I''ll leave this house and never come back, and you can eat your supper when you sweet please, and I'll eat mine when I please. There's the gang now, and I haven't had a bite to eat just because of your everlasting whining."

But, Matt dear, I—"

"Shut up, will you?"

"But I was only going to say—"

"I don't want to hear what you were going to say."

Great tears fell from the girl's eyes into the cup of coffee she was holding in her trembling hand.

"Here, Matt, drink this, please. I didn't mean to insult nor boss you. I am only trying to help you because I—I love you—because mother—"

She could not finish her sentence, but sobbing aloud she pointed to their mother's picture on the shelf.

For a moment Matt stared at the picture, then at his sister and just then the boys outside whistled.

He started for the door and instantly Emily was at his side with her arm around his dirty neck.

"Oh, Matt—Matt, I can't see you go. Oh, Matt, won't you stop drinking and stop running with that gang? Won't you, Matt? Oh, won't you answer your mother's prayers, and give your heart to God, Matt?"

An internal laugh shook his body. He shook off her slender arm and opened the door. The snow on the ground was several inches thick and long icicles hung from the telegraph wires.

"I'm goin', sis." He looked at her with a cruel, glassy stare. "I'm goin' to live my life as I please and you live yours in Church and prayer meetings if you please. Your friends don't suit me and mine don't suit you, so we'll just part for good. I'm goin' in the morning to—"

With that, he closed the door.

Emily stood with the cup of coffee still in her hand, stood paralyzed and dazed.

"Matt's going—never coming back—never? Eternal God—everlasting arms—"

The room grew dark, the clock stopped ticking, the air pressed in and Emily fell with a heavy thud upon the floor, her face buried in the broken pieces of the heavy hot cup.

How long she lay there, no one knows, but those everlasting arms must have reached down and lifted her up from the pool of blood. She reeled and tottered to the door of the adjoining apartment. She somehow made her way to the phone and called a doctor. When he came Emily was only half conscious and she never remembered being taken to his office, never remembered having stitches taken in an ugly cross-shaped gash on her right cheek.

***

Two weeks passed and Matt did not come back. Several days later Emily was seen leaving the house carrying a brown, battered traveling bag; on her right cheek was a patch of gauze.

A window in the flat above was raised and an old woman thrust her head out curiously.

"Where ye be goin', Miss Dune, honey?"

"I'm—I'm going away for awhile, Mrs. Littleton. I can't stand it since Matt left. I've sub-rented the rooms."

"I sure hate to see ye go, child. I'll miss them Church songs ye sang so pretty 'fore ye got hurt, and them Sunday school papers ye al'ays brung me. Ye look mighty peaked too. Goin' to relation?

"Good-bye, Mrs. Littleton." The girl's voice faltered. "I'll miss you too."

Something in her throat almost choked her. "God bless you and keep you. I'll mail the papers to you. And if Matt should—should come back tell him I—love him and he will find me and our Eternal God by the signs of the crosses."

"What ye mean, honey?"

Without answering, Emily followed the icy walk toward town. The old woman stayed by the open window until her friend, the dearest God had ever sent her, was out of sight.

"Tell Matt—" the old woman almost hissed as she poked the fire in the old coal stove. "If I ever see Matt Dune again I'll tell him a-plenty, so I will. How can that beautiful lily love that low down rascal?"

One stormy night three weeks later, Matt with sleeves rolled up and a butcher's apron on, was making hamburger sandwiches in the window of a dingy little lunchroom on a busy side street in Flint. His face was sunken and haggard, and his eyes were bloodshot. He seemed to be having a good time, however, talking and laughing with the man beside him who was cutting pie and pouring coffee for the long line of customers on the other side of the counter.

An old woman clad in a long black coat, a rustic old-fashioned bonnet, and a closely woven black veil, stopped in front of the lunchroom and stood close to the window as if to find shelter from the piercing wind. She stood for some time watching Matt flop the meat cakes on the greasy iron. Finally she opened her purse and counted her change, hesitated a moment, and went in. She took a table in the corner of the farthest corner of the room and ordered a sandwich and a cup of coffee.

"The sandwich without mustard, if you please, sir." Her voice was hesitant and a little trembly.

"One plain, Matt," laughed the waiter. "For your grandmother over there in the corner."

Matt answered with a louder laugh, and tossed the sandwich over the counter. The old woman had her back turned and did not see. She ate slowly as if she needed to sit and rest, and when she went out the door Matt thought he heard her give a low moan. He slapped the next meat cake on the iron while he cleared his throat emphatically. He didn't want to think of it again, but that moan reminded him of the way his mother moaned the first time she found out that he smoked.

"I hope she never comes in here again," he cursed under his breath. "This is no place for the feeble-minded to eat."

After Matt left the lunch room that night, he crossed the street and went into a pool room. After an hour he came out dragging his tired feet beneath him. He was breathing heavily. Taking a step forward awkwardly he all but knocked over that same old woman he had seen in the lunch room that evening.

"I beg your pardon," she said in a low, breathy tone. Matt only grunted and trudged on.

The next evening while Matt was frying the meat cakes in the window, he noticed that black-veiled woman again, only this time she looked more bent and more hideous.

"I hate her," he said to himself. "The very sight of her gives me the creeps."

"I saw your grandmother this morning, Matt," said the waiter a few days later. "Down on twenty-first street wheeling a baby cart for one of those wealthy folks. I sure wouldn't let that old woman take care of a baby of mine."

"Just so she stays there is all I care," answered Matt angrily. "And if you call her my grandmother again I'll finish up on you."

At that very moment the door opened and in stepped that queer figure. The men laughed and sneered and no one offered to wait on her. She stood with her one hand on the latch, her other hand holding a small white package. She hesitated, turned to go, then as if compelled, walked over toward Matt, laid the small package down on the counter in front of him and went out. With a whistle Matt tossed the package across the room to one of the men.

"Here's your birthday present, Jim. Look out, it might be poison."

Jim tore the paper and with a yell of delight thrust something yellow into his pocket, read what was printed on a small white slip and tore it into bits.

In an instant, Matt had hold of Jim. "Give me that, you fool." He had him by the throat and held him thus while he reached into his pocket and pulled out a crumpled ten dollar bill.

"Is this all of it?"

"All of it, you brute!"

"And what was on that white slip you tore up? Tell me! What?"

Jim did not answer. Grabbing his cap he walked out and did not return.

Matt stood dazed, bewildered. An almost terrified expression crossed his face.

He left the lunch room that evening at ten o'clock. The snow was falling, gently covering the icy walks with a thin blanket. He lit a cigarette and was crossing the street when his foot slipped and he fell directly in front of an approaching coal truck. The driver slammed on his brakes, his truck skidded, a woman screamed, and the motionless bleeding body of Matthew Dune lay under the truck.

People ran, people jammed, women screamed, policemen ordered and no one knew who it was that dashed into the nearest store, grabbed a phone and called an ambulance.

It was just driving away from the scene with Matt, when an old woman in a long black coat, a queer rustic bonnet draped with a veil darted to a man standing at the edge of the crowd, took him frantically by the arm and demanded, "Have you a car handy, sir?" The man jumped back as if struck. He nodded.

"Get into it quickly," her voice was strong and commanding. Without knowing why, the man walked quickly to his car and got in. The woman leaped into the front seat beside him. The man turned to her in dumb amazement.

"Follow that ambulance," she commanded, pointing a thin gloved hand to the slowly moving gray cab in the near distance. "I must get there. I will pay you."

***

From her pocket she took out a dollar bill and handed it to him. He was too astonished to take it. She thrust it into his vest pocket. Her breath came short and fast. She leaned forward in the seat and watched the gray car ahead of them like a tamer watches the eyes of a tiger. Twice, her body shook convulsively, and she said something in an undertone that the driver could not understand.

It was an hour before the door of the operating room was opened and the sleeping man under the long white cover was wheeled slowly to a room at the end of the second floor and placed in bed. And by special permission, after much hesitation, the woman who had followed Matt there was allowed to sit in the corner of the room while the nursed stayed by the bed.

It was after one when one of Matt's hands moved nervously and he made a faint moan. Instantly the old woman in the corner of the room stood up, made a faint cry as of relief, then dropped on her knees by the window.

In the very stillest part of the night, when every living creature seems to be asleep, and every moving object motionless, and the darkness is its darkest, and the diamonds in the snow under the street lights sparkle, and dance fairy-like, Matt opened his eyes, looked straight into the face of the nurse, felt the pain in his legs and his head, and knew where he was. He KNEW where he was.

The realization of everything past and present stood before him like a map. He could follow distinctly the road he had taken from the time his mother first whipped him, to the moment he fell in the street several hours ago. Then it hovered over him in a boiling, foaming, tangled mass; it came down around him closer and closer, closing in upon him; it strangled, choked, smothered, buried him. It grew red, purple, black, thick black. It was killing him. He saw as in a dream his mother and Emily with radiant faces, not aware of his condition, not trying to help him. Then he saw Emily as she stood with the cup of coffee in her hand, her auburn falling in pretty waves around her sweet sad face, her blue gingham apron, the table set for two, Emily's eyes. In a flash Matt lived again every action and word of that night. "Oh, Matt, won't you answer mother's prayers and give your heart to God?" These words cut him now like a knife. With a shriek the man cried out, "My God, I will," and smote his trembling hand to his breast. The nurse jumped as though struck and caught the man's hand.

"You are—"

"Listen nurse," his voice was begging, but faint and unsteady. "Send a telegram at once to Miss Emily Dune in Markville, please."

"And what will it be?"

"Come. Go at once please. Oh—Emily, God help her—Emily."

"Go—go. I am all right—Jesus!"

The nurse left the room. Out of the shadowy corner of the room rose the old woman who had sunken there in a half-faint. Slowly she measured her way, inch by inch across the room. Silently she slipped up beside the bed and stood there watching the face of the man whose eyes were closed.

A pitiful cry shook his big body and he opened his eyes and saw again that hideous black-veiled figure.

"What—what are you doing here?" His voice was husky and trembling. "Are you a ghost or—or what do you want of me? I never harmed you. I—I—the money—I am dreaming,"

"The old woman took hold of the corner of the veil and slowly lifted it up over her rustic bonnet.

"No—no—God, my God. Emily—my sister—no. What is that on your cheek?"

He closed his eyes and covered his face with his hand. A terrible, stifled sob shook his entire body.

"My—cross—Matt. Do not let it frighten you. I know it makes me look ugly. That's why I wear the veil—and—"

"But Emily, oh, dear, how did it happen—when—?"

"It's all right, Matt. Just after you left—I—you know I had a cup in my hand."

"No—no, Emily." Great tears came into Matt's eyes and he cried as few men ever do. He caught her hands and pulled her face down to his own and kissed that cross-shaped scar over and over again.

"And you are the woman I made fun of in the lunch room? And you are the woman I refused to wait on this morning and you are the one the fellows called my grandmother, and you're that angel who brought me that ten dollar bill this morning to spend on drink and cigarettes—my sister?"

"Not for drink, Matt. Didn't you read what was on the white slip?"

"I didn't see the slip."

"Why, Matt, I'm sure I put it in."

"What was on it, Emily?"

It's all right now, Matt. I saw you needed a new coat."

She had removed her long black coat now, and the old-fashioned bonnet, and stood by the bed, the Emily of two months ago, tell slender, beautiful, her auburn hair falling in soft waves around her sweet sad face; but not the same Emily, for her eyes were sunken and dark, her cheeks were colorless and—the scar!

"Oh, Emily. I—you—you." Matt could not talk. He could only clasp her hands and wash them in his tears. "You love me enough to—"

"I would have followed you to the end of the world, Matt, to lead you to the cross."

"You have followed me through—God!" Matt felt the sharp pain in his head, groaned, and lost his consciousness.

When he opened his eyes again the first gray rays of dawn were creeping timidly into the room. He looked at Emily, who was kneeling by the bed, her saintly face lifted toward heaven. He placed his finger tips gently on the ugly scar and prayed. "Oh, Father, 'the way of the cross leads home' I follow." She smiled the smile that recompenses for all pain and sorrow, that makes the burden of the cross light with the glory of the vision of the crown.

"Emily, how long have you been following me?"

"Almost a month, Matt. I saw you often before I came in to eat. I saw you every day. Oh, Matt—Matt don't. You must go to sleep now, please. We will talk again when you are rested."

"Ill never close my eyes again until I know you are asleep first, Emily."

The nurse who had been standing outside the door for some time stepped in.

"Here is your nurse now, Matt. I'll go to sleep right away."

How's That?

By Christmas Carol Kauffman, age 36, Hannibal Missouri
Originally published May 21 and 28, 1939
in the Youth's Christian Companion

Some men are handsome and some are good-looking; that is they just look as though they were made up of those qualities which, when blended together, make a man look good, because they are manifested on his face, in his walk, and in his very being.

Dan McAfee was not handsome. His eyes were rather small; his hair scant and streaked with gray; his nose too large to be artistic; and on his left cheek he wore a deep scar. But in spite of all this, Dan McAfee looked good. He had a good man's looks, because behind his scarred face, lay a good heart. He was so kind, so patient, so considerate of others, not only members of his own family but also of every other one. He was always happy and contented, though a hard-working man, and blessed with only a small portion of this world's goods. He had buried three children, all less than ten years of age. That was years ago.

Mrs. McAfee was a quiet little woman who minded her own business, and was very industrious. In spite of his many needs, Dan McAfee still had a few things to make him happy, although others couldn't see it.

Across the fence stood a large frame house not over fifteen years old. John Crockett lived there; that is, he stayed there part of the time. Now he was what the world called a handsome young man. He lacked nothing for outward appearance—tall, straight and clever.

"Hi, John," Dan McAfee was taking the clothes line down for his good wife and was winding up the tail as he neared the iron fence. "Hi, Mr. McAfee," answered John politely. The song he was whistling stopped in the middle of the sentence and seemed to hang trembling above his head.

"Been working hard today?"

"Oh, not too hard, John. There was a time when I worked too hard, though."

"When you worked by the piece?" John came close to the fence, hands in pockets. He kicked a little snow off the point of his shoe.

"When I worked—" Mr. McAfee tied the end of the line, then looked John straight in the eyes, "for the devil," he finished.

John blushed very slightly. "How's that?" he laughed softly.

"Well the harder I worked the more he whipped me an' demanded me to work still harder'; an' the harder I worked the more he promised to pay me. But one night I saw him make out a check for my friend who worked beside me, an' the check was DEATH!" Dan McAfee's eyes, though small, burned suddenly like two glowing embers, and his breath came fast and hard.

John Crocker stood speechless. "How's that?" The words came through his teeth in a loud whisper.

"Well, sir," Dan McAfee shifted from one foot to the other and a sweet seriousness crossed his honest face, "did you ever see a sinner die?"

"I never saw anybody die."

"Well," continued Mr. McAfee slowly, "Ed Pullian wasn't a bit more wicked than I was. He wouldn't have killed a man if he was fightin' mad any sooner that I would have. He cussed, an' drank, an' chewed, an' smoked, an' raised Cain around home, an' lied as fast as he talked, an' took advantage of his neighbors, an' squandered his money faster 'n he made it, gambled, an' done all the other crooked things a crooked man'll do. Well, sir, we worked side by side at the foundry over at Lakeville; that was back in 1873. James was a little chap about five, an' Lottie a wee thing that couldn't walk, yet. Well, sir, Ed always said when a man died, he died like an animal. He wasn't afraid of nothin'. He made fun of his sisters who worried the Lord with their many prayers, an' said how he didn't have time to fool with the church, an' the Bible was a myth, an' so on. I agreed with him; or at least I told him I did, for I thought it was smart. But I couldn't help believin' all the while that my mother had gone to heaven,; for she always talked of goin' there when she died.

"One day Ed took sick all at once like, an' had to go home—had to be taken home, couldn't even walk. He didn't come to work for two days, so I went to see him. Partly paralyzed he was, an' I said. 'Ed, this is tough.' An' he said, 'I know it, Dan.' I said,'You won't draw a full-time pay check this week, will you?' An' the queerest look I ever saw crossed his face.

"Just then his wife spoke up an' said, 'He's been talkin' out of his head all afternoon, Mr. McAfee. He thinks the boss was here an' gave him his check—paid him off in full.' She whispered it like to me. An' all at once, Ed, he, half sat up, an' his eyes got glassy, an' as big as could be. An' he picked up something beside his pillow an' showed it to me (only there wasn't a thing in his hand), an' said, 'Here's my pay check, Dan, for all my hard work. Nothin' but DEATH—death! He moaned an' fell back on his pillow, an' gave one horrible cry an' was gone—that imaginary check still clenched in his big fist!

"Such an expression on his face! Such agony I never hope to see again. The undertaker tried to fix him up, but he couldn't. That look never left him. An' that night after I got home, I—"

"John, oh, John!" Someone called from the large house.

"Yes."

"Telephone."

"O.K." John ran into the house.

"Say, Dan," Mrs. McAfee spoke gently as she took the cornbread from the oven, "you'll take a cold if you stand out there by the house so long without your cap. See."

"Maybe so, dear. I'll try to remember that. Cornbread tonight, um?"

"Does that suit you?" she smiled timidly, teasingly.

"You know me by this time, don't you, Polly?" He patted her cheek tenderly.

"I ought to," she blushed like a girl, and fumbled with the handkerchief in her apron pocket. "I know you're a good man, and I love to make you what you like."

"How do you know I'm a good man?"

"Someone knocked, Dan."

On the porch stood a little girl in a red coat and cap, a market basket in one hand. When she smiled, deep dimples (where an angel must have kissed her) made her babyish and sweeter than ever.

"Would you like to buy some sugary popcorn, Mister?"

"Sugary popcorn?" Dan McAfee smiled fatherly. "Now what kind is that, my little lady?"

"Well, it's gooder than straight, plain, popcorn; you know. Mother puts sugar on while it pops; and when it's done, it's all sugary."

"You don't say? Come inside. Let me see this wonderful popcorn."

The child stepped inside and Mr. McAfee took a paper sack out and opened it.

"You say your mother makes this?"

"Yes, sir."

"For you to sell?"

"Yes, sir."

"How much is it?"

"Ten cents."

"Only ten cents for such a sack full?"

"Yes, sir."

"Then I must try some. Don't you think so, Mother?"

"I think we can buy a sack." She smiled at the tiny miss. "You're not out alone, are you, dear?"

The child nodded.

"But it's soon dark, child."

The child nodded again.

"What's your name, Little Sister?"

"Nancy."

"Nancy what?"

"Nancy Christine."

"Is Christine your last name?"

"No, sir. All my name is Nancy Christine"—she hesitated. She started again. "Nancy Christine Noble,'" she gave her little red-capped head a jerk.

"Is it hard to remember?"

She nodded.

In spite of himself, Dan McAfee let out a hearty laugh. It seemed so utterly impossible that such a clever child should forget her name.

"Well—you—you—see," she stammered shyly. "I have a new name since yesterday. An' I can't hardly remember it, yet."

"A new name! How's that?"

"Mother got married." She rather frowned a little.

Oh, she was so little to be having something to worry about. The big kind heart of Dan McAfee was touched with a strange feeling. He somehow wanted to take that child and fold her in his strong arms. "But you should keep your own name, Nancy. What was your father's name?"

"I daresn't never say it." She looked frightened. Her big eyes look all around and behind her.

"Why?"

"He said so."

"Who said so?"

"He—Mr. Noble did."

"But he has no right." Dan's face colored.

"Sh—"   Mrs. McAfee touched Dan on the arm. "Let it go."

"But that's not right, Polly. You know it." He insisted. "Tell me your real name, Honey."

"She shook her head. "I don't want a beatin'. I want a new doll an'—"

"Where do you live, Little Sister?" Dan got down on one knee and looked up into her blessed face.

"I don't know the street's name. It's down that way past a little bridge an' back that way jus' past that big green house."

"That's an empty lot if I remember right."

"Well, we live in a trailer house. It's getting' dark an' I must go."

"Here's your dime, Honey. Now run along, an' come back again."

"O.K.," she smiled and tripped away just a bundle of red beside a basket. A minute later Dan McAfee heard a man's husky voice call, "Nancy?"

The child stopped as if struck. She looked this way and that, then suddenly dropped her basket on the sidewalk and looking in the direction of the iron fence clapped her hands frantically, half laughing, half crying, "Oh! Oh!" and made a dash across the yard.

"Dan," called Mrs. McAfee from the table when she was pouring the water, now, "please answer that phone."

"Yes, Polly." He had not heard it.

"Who was it?"

"Oh, Freds. They're comin' over for a friendly call after a while."

"Well, then, let's eat." She pulled up the chairs. "It's almost six already."

The blessing was asked with reverence. As Dan McAfee passed the bread, he said, "I wonder who called that little girl. Someone over the fence. Then the phone and—and after that she was gone." He scratched his head. "I didn't hear it."

"Dan," spoke his wife near the end of the meal. "Dan, what's on your mind?"

"That little Nancy Christine—er whatever her name is. I can't forget her."

"You're always tryin' to work out some problem for someone else," she chuckled softly.

"Well, you know me," he smiled.

***

Four days later John Crocker and Dan McAfee met by chance on the corner. Dan was coming from the store with a quart of milk in one hand.

"Fine evening, John."

"Very fine," answered John. He stroked his silky hair.

"Been workin' hard, today?"

John looked away for a moment. "Not too hard, I guess," he smiled quite bravely, quite splendidly. He wanted to go, but something kept him. He remembered the conversation by the house a few nights before and recalled with quite an unpleasant memory one sleepless night and after that strange dreams.

"I see by the paper your boss lost his wife this morning," continued Mr. McAfee.

"Yes." John stroked his hair. He has a way of doing that often.

"Died suddenly, didn't she?"

"Must have." John tried again to go, but his feet seemed to be frozen to the cement walk. He was ashamed of himself. He would take himself in hand.

"Well, I hope she was ready an' received her gift."

"Say," John began. "I've been—a—wanting to ask you a question." He looked down.

"Go ahead. I'll answer if I can."

"Well, if that—that Ed, I believe you called him," John fumbled nervously with some loose change in his pocket.

"Ed Pullian?"

"Yes, I believe that's what you called him. Well, say, if he was delirious when he told you all that, then how do you know—" John hesitated.

"Know what?"

"Well, listen." John threw back his head, "how do you know that's what he really got?"

"Because I know. The Good Book says so. In Romans 6:23 it says, 'For the wages of sin is death, but the gift of God is eternal life through Jesus Christ our Lord'."

"Well, then, have you ever seen a good man die?"

"Several."

Dan McAfee saw the question on the young man's face and hurried to answer it. "It was altogether different from Ed. Pullian's death, too. A triumphant passing over into that glory world." As the man spoke, his scarred face shone with a radiance almost divine. As John Crocker, head and shoulders above his neighbor, stood there on the corner he felt suddenly mean and food-for-nothing. Could Mr. McAfee know that inside he was miserable and—and afraid? Could he tell how hard it had been to shake off those things he had told him? He despised himself for being such a sissy. He would go to his room, shave, and go to the movie, and smoke, and laugh it off. Yes, he would. Bash these silly fairy tales, these crazy superstitious things weak-minded folks say they believe. It was absurd and ridiculous. Again he stroked his lovely black hair.

"Well, I s'pose your good wife has patiently been waiting for that milk."

"Yes, I must go. You go home and read that for yourself, John. Well—" there was surprise in his voice—" there comes my little popcorn lady down the hill."

John caught his breath. A peculiar sound escaped his lips. He coughed.

"Oh!" A stifled moan escaped Dan McAfee's throat, and he ran toward the street above him. John outran the older man. The child had slipped on the icy pavement and struck her head on the curbing. Popcorn lay all around her. A big coal truck just missed her legs.

The next moment she was in John Crocker's arm with her face close to his.

"Nancy, are you hurt, Sweetheart?" Dan heard him say.

"My head!" She tried to smile through her tears. "The popcorn is all spilled. "Oh!" Now she really did cry.

"Don't worry about the popcorn, Nancy as long as you're not badly hurt."

"But he'll beat—"

"He will not beat you, Honey."

"He—he did," she sobbed.

John's arms tightened around her body, and he put a kiss on her wet cheek.

"I don't care what he said. This was an accident and we both saw it."

"Certainly. I, Dan McAfee, saw it, too, and I'll go along home with you and tell your father so. You couldn't help it, and so don't cry, Honey. I'll pay for part of it."

Just then a car stopped. "Child hurt?" a man asked anxiously.

"Not bad," John answered.

"I thought at first it was someone I knew.   The red coat. Need any help?"

"No, thanks."

"Carry her over to our house." Dan McAfee led the way.

"Where's my Daddy?" she looked up into John Crocker's face pleadingly.

"Oh, child!" He stumbled to the nearest chair with a groan. "I wish I knew for sure." This he said to Dan McAfee. "Mr. McAfee," John's voice trembled, "This is my brother's child. He was taken away two years ago to a hospital (that's what they always t-o-l-d   N-a-n-c-y)." John spelled out the words and "p-e-n."

Dan nodded recognition.

"DEAD!" Tears came into John Crocker's eyes. "That —check business! Oh, if I only knew! I'm afraid." He shook his head and held Nancy close.

"Noble's a scoundrel. It nearly kills me."

"She has to go by the name 'Noble,' she says," Dan's voice was husky.

"How's that?"

"He—he said—he'd beat me if I ever tell anyone my name is Nancy Crocker," she cried pitifully.

"He will?"

"But Crocker is your name just the same. Your mother did not know I lived in this town, did she? And next door to a man who buys popcorn? Well, I saw you on Monday night. You are too little to be peddling. You poor, dear, child. Jason would—" he caught his breath. He dare not talk about it now.

"Something should be done." This Mr. McAfee said.

"It's going to be done as soon as we put a little medicine on her head. Not bad, is it?"

If ever a young man showed determination on his face John Crocker did just then.

"What are you going to do, John?" asked Dan McAfee.

"Well—" John took a deep breath. "First of all I'm going to start—start working for a new Boss; then a lot—a lot of other things will work out for themselves."

Dan McAfee grabbed John by the hand and pressed it.

"How's that, Mr. McAfee?"

"You're on the right track, my boy. God bless you. He will be a real Boss and 'the gift of God is eternal life.' Oh, John, I'm glad you see it while you're young."

"Well, Mr. McAfee, I've been seeing a lot since you talked to me out there by the fence; and Jason's life, and Nancy —oh! I've been doing a lot of thinking, sir! And now it's time to act before I get paid off."

"God bless you, Son." Dan McAfee's face shone with new joy.

Say It With ?

By Christmas Carol Kauffman, age 41, Hannibal, Missouri
Originally published Aug 13, 1944 in the Youth's
Christian Companion

A talk given to the girls of Hesston College,
January 31, 1944, which will be appreciated by every
reader, especially the girls.

You have all seen the florists' nationwide slogan, "Say it with flowers." The florists have adopted that slogan because it says exactly what they want to say in the fewest possible words. The florist knows that in his shop he has something that can carry a message to anyone—young or old, rich or poor, any kind, any size, any price. You come in and you select what you want. He'll fix it up. You put your name on a card. He ties it on and sends it for you. You say it with flowers. Say what? Say "it." What is "it?" The "it" depends on the sender.

When a young man sends his lady love a bouquet of lovely red roses, what could it say but "I love you"? What young man would spend money for roses for a girl he didn't love. He says "it" with flowers and she understands.

When a girl sends her mother roses for Mother's Day, they say "it"—the flowers do. They say, "Mother, I think you're wonderful. No other mother like you. No one else would do." You do not need to write it all out. The flowers say it for you. She understands.

When one of your classmates has to go to Newton to the hospital and stay awhile, you get together and send her flowers. They have a way of saying "it" like nothing else could. They say, "We all miss you. We can hardly wait till you are back with us again. Please obey the doctor's orders and get well soon!" You don't write it all out. There is no need to. The flowers say it all for you.

When someone you love dies, you might send flowers to the home. You only put your name on a card, or maybe just hand it to them without a card. The flowers say what you never could for choking. They might say volumes no pen could write. They have a language all their own.

When the city hospital in Hannibal was dedicated, different business firms sent out baskets of lowers. The flowers said "it." They said "We appreciate your patronage. We wish you success. Call on us again."

Some time ago an evangelist from a distance was holding meetings in Hannibal. One morning the doorbell rang, and a boy handed me a package with this man's name on it. It was a beautiful bouquet of snapdragons. It was his birthday, but we didn't know it until then. It was from his home folks. As soon as he read the names he knew what the flowers told him. They said, "We all love you. You know it's more than words can tell, and we're all for you. Success in your meetings. Do your level best." The flowers said all that, and a lot more. The florists couldn't have chosen a better slogan.

When a beautiful little girl tiptoes into the schoolroom squeezing a straggly little bouquet she gathered along the way, and hands it up to her teacher, what does it say? What could it say but "I like you, teacher—but I'm too bashful to tell you so." The flowers say it for her. The teacher gets the message.

It's nice to get flowers, and it's nice to send them, but not many of us can afford to be ordering cut flowers from the florists very often. Not many of you girls get roses sent out from Newton every week, do you?

The florist's slogan, "Say it with flowers," took hold on me one day as I was passing the flower shop. I stopped to admire the delicate beauty of them all, and wished for a moment I could afford to send flower messages to many friends I loved. I thought of several invalids who very seldom get flowers, I thought of several friends who had recently been bereft of loved ones. After everything's all over with, wouldn't it be nice to send flowers to tell them "someone is still sympathizing." Then I thought of my father who so tenderly cared for Mother on her long illness. Flowers could tell him how I admired him for his faithfulness. Then there was a girl who was being graduated. I would have liked to send her flowers with congratulations. But that daydream would never come true—and you know it. But as I stood there I thought how like flowers people are. Every kind of flower in the window reminded me of someone, yes, even the cosmos and bright marigolds. "I'll have to say what I want to say without flowers," I thought.

Do you know we say "it" every day. Say what? We're saying "it" but not with flowers. Every girl has longings, some are too serious and sacred to mention to anyone but a very confidential friend. Some of you long to succeed in your Christian life and be a credit to God and the church. Some of you long to make good in some vocation, and most, if not all of you, secretly long to have a home of your own some day.

Why do some girls' dream come true, and others do not? What makes some girls win their way into the lives of others, and some get pushed back? What makes some girls very attractive and popular, and others feel sensitive and shy? Is it the kind of home a girl comes from? It can't be that only because some of the loveliest girls come from homes of modest means. Some of the prettiest flowers grow back in the bush. Is it the clothes a girl wears? No, because some of the best dressed are the least loved. Is it the size or shape of a girl, or the complexion or the color of hair or is it the way she walks sings, or talks that makes her attractive? No doubt everyone of you has asked yourself these questions many times. Some girls just have a way of making folks love them—but what is it? Why do some win the respect of others, and some do not?

God made everything that is beautiful, not only the flowers but also birds and babies—and girls. Many women in their desperation to make themselves beautiful have made a first class failure of it. Thousands of girls today are making bouquets out of themselves ready to be delivered to any man who will receive them. But the sad part is this: the very thing they think they are saying is just what they are not saying. The woman who goes down the street in the summertime with a fur around her neck, and scantily clad in the winter thinks she is saying "it." She thinks she is saying, "See how attractive I am," but in reality she is saying, "How very inconsistent I am." The girl who paints her fingernails and lips and plucks her eyebrows, and shows her bare knees to everyone, thinks she is saying "it." She wants to say, "Don't you think I'm cute?" But in reality she is saying, "I'm fickle and whimsical and changeable, and as soon as the style changes, I will too." The girl who makes up with boys easily, and flirts with every Tom, Dick, and Harry, and every soldier on the road, thinks she is a lovely bouquet saying "it." She thinks she is saying, "I'm a good sport. Everybody thinks I'm a darling." But in reality she is saying quite the opposite. She is saying, "I am treacherous, and dishonest. I am not pure, not reliable, and no one can trust me, not even myself." The girl who smokes and reads the popular news-stand magazines, and fixes her hair in the latest extreme fashion, thinks she is saying, "I'm not one of those drab old maids. Ask me for a date. I'll show you a swell time. I'll even drink a little if you want me to." She thinks she's a peony saying "it'." But in reality she is saying, "I'm empty and shallow. I'm just a make-believe, and I'm always jittery and nervous."

Rev. Parks Cadman said after he had seen how some girls act today, "Nobody is going to look at a face all his life, that once was only a piece of rock salt for every calf to lick that came down the road."

Every girl on this campus is saying "it," not with flowers, but by her actions, and attitudes, and dress. No matter how talented or wealthy a girl may be, she may be saying some very ugly, mean, and ignorant things. No matter how poor a girl may seem, she may be saying some very lovely things.

"Love is the going out of one soul to another. It's the perfume of life. Do we leave a perfume like a rose or like a marigold? Everyone is saying something.

A girl's speech betrays what she is. No noble boy admires a loud, vulgar, boisterous, slangy girl. Say "it" with refined, moderate speech. Men do not like a slouchy girl with ill-kept hair and nails. A girl that is careless about her dress is careless about her room. Say "it" with neat, modest clothes.

Men like girls with cheerful dispositions, girls that can smile at the right time, but who don't titter and giggle at everything. A cranky, grouchy, complaining girl is never attractive. Some girls feel depressed because of ill health. One can become easily discouraged when suffering from some bodily ailment. A girl can never stay out late at night eating hamburgers and candy, drinking pop, and lose sleep, then get up in the morning fresh as a daisy. Some girls get up after such a night and feel cross without knowing why. They can't eat breakfast. They kick the cat and scold sister. Some girls get silly and light because they don't have enough to do.

A happy, cheerful girl is a busy girl that doesn't have time to hold her hands. Then some girls have too much to do, and are overloaded with duties. They hardly find time to read, or pray, and get irritable easily and do not know why.

Say "it" with a cheery face and a do-something-worthwhile air. Men don't like girls that never take anything seriously, but who are serious enough to respect the rights and feelings of others. Jealousy is a terrible monster that works havoc in the finest lives sometimes. Jealousy can ruin a girl spiritually, physically, and mentally. No amount of pills can cure her. The Lord only can undertake such a case.

Say "it" with a kind and serious manner. Men like girls that have a reasonable amount of self-confidence. Some girls are afflicted with an inferiority complex that puts a shadow over their lives. They feel afraid and ashamed, and have an idea that everybody misjudges them, and that they are a misfit everywhere. God can marvelously undertake for any girl who is tortured with an inferiority complex. Say "it" with a moderate amount of self-confidence, but with a reliance on God. Men like girls who don't worry easily. Worry stifles a girl's life. It takes the bloom from her cheeks. It makes her steps slow and draggy. It takes the sparkle and snap out of her eyes. and brings lines in her face. Some girls worry all day and go to sleep worrying, and dream about something to worry about the next day. There's only one cure for the fretter, and that's the Lord. Christ could have worried all his life about His horrible death, but He didn't. Say "it" with a calm and quiet heart that tells you to trust God.

Men like girls who have noble character. Character is what we are in the dark, when no one else is around. Men like girls that are getting ready to make real women. Say "it" with a ladylike deportment. Where do you stand today, girls? Are you getting away from God who will help your life to be a perfume and a blessing to others. Today, as never before, the devil is tempting our young women to be fickle—to have that, I don't care attitude. He tempts every girl to lie, flirt, and follow the crazy crowd.

Say "it" with an honest, pure heart. Some girls today are trying desperately to hide a heart that's in the depths of self-condemnation so that they can hardly laugh it off any longer. It keeps a girl from acting natural. Some girls are lonely, and suffering in a strange way, because they have to take a stand alone for what they believe. Sometimes it's hard to keep praising God when you feel alone. But say "it" if you must stand alone. Say "it" with Christian assurance. Don't let any well-meaning person tell you to brace up, or pull yourself together. You can't do it. If you are trying to cover secret sin, or are jealous, or lonely, or have an inferiority complex, or have been shallow or giddy or disobedient or proud, there is only one way out, and that's by letting Jesus Christ do "it" for you.

Instead of sending your president and dean flowers on their birthdays, why not say "it" tomorrow and every day with true Christian co-operation. Say "it" with honesty. Tell them you're here to make Hesston a better place, but don't try to say it with flowers. Say it by your conduct.

Your being—your character—is saying something. It's saying "it." What is "it" you are saying? Be sure you are saying what you want to say.

After the Flood

By Christmas Carol Kauffman, age 49, Hannibal, Missouri
Originally published March 2, 1952
in the Youth's Christian Companion

Daniel slipped in late. Quickly he walked to his seat by the east window looking at no one, not even the teacher. He knew she was looking at him, for this was the third time he'd been tardy this week. The sixth grade pupils were already reciting their history lesson. His chest hurt from running up over the hill. Quickly he got out his history book and found the page.

Miss Foster asked Daniel the next question. He was embarrassed and confused. He shook his head.

"You may stay after school then," Miss Foster's voice was firm.

Daniel felt the warmness creep over his face. He felt every eye in the room riveted on him. This would please Joe Mattson. He gloried when ever any boy had to be reprimanded or punished. Secretly Joe hoped Daniel Holliday would have to write the names of all the presidents as often as he had had to write them the night before. Joe chuckled inside.

Daniel bit his lip and looked down. He opened up his notebook and picked up his pencil, but his heart was still thumping madly.

At recess, Daniel lingered in the room. Shyly he walked up to his teacher.

"Couldn't I do it now, Miss Foster?"

"Do what?"

"What you wanted me to stay in for tonight?"

"Why now? Why can't you stay in tonight as I told you to?"

Daniel's soft sad eyes touched her somehow.

"I—I just can't."

Miss Foster dared not let her feelings give way.

"But, you—you must stay. I—I simply cannot have you being tardy so often. You will have to be punished. It's too nice to be in this morning. You need the fresh air and so do I. And I'm not used to having my pupils tell me what they will or will not do. You may go out now and play with the other children."

But as she spoke she placed a hand gently on his shoulder.

Daniel drew a long deep breath. Suddenly his lip quivered and his eyes that looked straight at Miss Foster were full of tears.

"Why, Daniel Holliday," she whispered, "what on earth is wrong? I wish you would just come right out and tell me. I can't understand."

He shifted his glance and fumbled nervously with a piece of string in his overall pocket.

"I have to help my father. Please—I have to go straight home tonight. I cannot stay."

"But why do you come tardy so often? I can't have it. Don't you have a clock at your house?"

"We do, but it doesn't work any more."

"Then how do you know what time it is?"

"I go by the train whistle, but this morning I didn't hear it."

"Were you listening for it?"

"I don't know. I—I"

"You mean you don't even care if you're late?"

"Oh, yes I care—I—I care, Miss Foster."

"Then explain, Daniel. Please tell me. This distresses me."

"Well," Daniel shifted from one foot to the other. "I have to work."

"What kind of work?"

"Everything."

"Everything like what?"

Joe Mattson stuck his head in the open door. "Come on out, Dandy Dan."

Daniel paid no attention.

Joe whistled between his fingers. "Come on out, Dandy Dan—play ball."

Miss Foster snapped her finger. "You run along, Joe," she called, "I'm talking with Daniel."

"Now listen to me," she began again, "did it go this way last year—I mean coming tardy so often?"

"No, ma'am. My father wasn't so—so bad then."

"Is your father sick in bed?"

"Yes, ma'am."

"There's no one to help with the work?"

"No, ma'am."

"Isn't your mother able?"

"I haven't any mother, Miss Foster."

"Oh, I—I didn't know that, Daniel," she whispered tenderly. "I'm sorry. I didn't know. Get out your history book and come up to my desk. I'll see if I can let you off this time."

Around Daniel's eyes the teacher had noticed a likeness to someone. In her six months of teaching in the hills of the Ozarks she had noticed it several times before. She watched him as he came timidly toward her. But what absurd thoughts. Mildred Foster shook herself chidingly. She had often seen faces that reminded her of someone else.

She went over the history lesson with Daniel, now and then placing her one hand on his shoulder. There was something so tender and likeable about him.

On Friday afternoon, the regular time for story hour, Miss Foster went outside to get a drink while the entire school finished studying spelling.

Far in the west the sky looked strange.

Joe Mattson reached over and socked Daniel in the head with his big green geography. Several big boys snickered, but everyone held his breath when Miss Foster walked in the door.

"You may stay after school, Joe," she said, "I saw that."

"Oh, shucks," growled Joe under his breath.

"That will do, Joe. Now today," she began, "I'm going to tell instead of read you a story."

"Oh, goody," clapped little Mary.

"Fold your hands and sit up straight. This is a true story. It happened in a small city in Missouri. This city is built right on the Mississippi river. Quite frequently, especially in the spring, the river gets very high when snow and ice begin to melt in the north, as we have studied in our geography classes. When the river gets high it causes floods. Hundreds of families who live in the lowlands have to move out of their homes and stay out sometimes for weeks." The teacher paused, then continued her story.

One family who lived in these lowlands had many children; one was a tiny baby.

The flood waters came up inch by inch until they reached the steps of their house. Then it began to rain. It rained for two days. The creek became swollen. There was water both in front of and behind their house.

The father and mother became frantic.

They piled their family into their old open truck and started off. They didn't know where to go. It was still raining hard; all the children were getting soaked.

The mother thought about the mission Sunday school where the children attended occasionally. The father drove up to the minister's home beside the church and hesitated. Then he dashed out through the rain, ran up onto the porch, rang the doorbell, and laid the baby down by the door. Then he ran back to the truck and drove off.

A woman looking out of her window across the street recognized the family and truck. After it drove away she noticed the bundle on the porch. She knew the minister and his wife were away attending a conference.

She watched. She saw the bundle move a little and a big dog run up on the porch and sniff all around the bundle.

She ran across the street and up onto the porch. The baby, damp and cold, was crying.

"Shall I stop here and continue with the story next week?"

"No," shouted forty voices in unison.

Mildred Foster smiled faintly. "The woman from across the street took the baby home. Of course, she couldn't leave it there on the porch for a dog to sniff over. She decided to keep it until the minister and his wife returned.

"But by that time, this woman, her husband, and children all fell in love with that little baby boy. They named him Leo."

Daniel's chin went up. He blinked twice. Miss Foster continued. "They wanted to keep the little fellow. The parents never came back to ask about the baby. When the minister and his wife came home, they were glad the neighbors had taken care of him.

"Two years passed and no one ever inquired about the baby, so these neighbors legally adopted him.

"The little boy was a very lonely child. He grew up to be a fine, promising young man. One day—"

The teacher caught her breath and held it.

"Oh, children!" Miss Foster's cheeks turned pale as she glanced out of the window. "I do believe a tornado is coming. Quick! Let us all go to the basement. Hurry. But don't jam."

The room grew dark. The schoolhouse rocked, and with the wind came a roaring sound with a strange whistle. The instant the last child and the teacher reached the bottom step, the corner of the schoolhouse roof was torn off and sent flying through the air. It landed in the clover field three hundred rods away.

It was over almost as quickly as it had come. Frightened children, wide-eyed and trembling, clung close to their teacher. They followed her up the stairs.

"Let's all bow our heads right here," she said, "and thank God for keeping us." In a voice full of fervency Mildred Foster offered a prayer of thanksgiving and sent the children home. She herself hurried to the home where she stayed. Two trees in the front yard had been uprooted.

"I'd like to ask a favor of you, Mr. Beck," began Mildred the next morning at breakfast.

Sure. What is it?"

"I'd like to borrow Doc."

"Borrow Doc?" Mr. Beck scratched his head. "What fer?"

"I'd like to ride horseback to visit one of my pupils."

"Yeh? Which one?"

"The Holliday boy."

"The Holliday boy? Goin' way out there, Miss Foster?"

"Why not?"

"Well, I've heard some strange things about the man, although I don't know him well at all. Met him only once an' he wasn't easy to talk with. Awful distant or somethin'."

"I felt I should go, Mr. Beck. I'm curious to know if there home was damaged."

"Better not go alone way in there, Miss Foster." ventured Mrs. Beck.

"Daniel will be there. I'm going to see him. I'm not one bit afraid."

"Sure thing you can have Doc. Go on ahead. She's easy ridin'," and Mr. Beck went straight toward the barn.

Mildred Foster had no trouble finding the Holliday place.

Daniel looked up in surprise as he heard the horse's hoofs on the lane behind the house.

"Someone is coming, Father," he whispered.

"Who could it be, Dan?"

Daniel looked out the kitchen window.

"Why, it's Miss Foster, my teacher, Father. Don't be worried."

He was at the door before she knocked.

"Good morning, Daniel."

"Good morning."

"I brought you an alarm clock."

"Oh, you didn't need to bring it, Miss Foster."

"I wanted to, Daniel. How is your dad this morning?"

"He's—" the boy looked troubled and twisted one finger around the other. "He's sorta bad today."

"I see your home wasn't damaged. I'm glad. May I come in just a minute?"

"Well—I—I guess so. I don't have all the work done up yet. I've been—"

"That's all right, Daniel. Maybe I can help you with the work. I'd like to meet your father."

In the corner of the meagerly furnished room lay the man on the bed, his one thin hand across his forehead.

"I'm—I'm Daniel's—" Mildred Foster stopped breathing. "Leo!" she cried. Leo—why—you—you—do know me, Leo?"

"Mildred," whispered the man feebly. "Of course, I know you. I've known it all the time, but—"

"But what, Leo? This seems almost impossible. Tell me if you can. You're not too sick to tell me, are you?"

He pointed at the startled wide-eyed boy at the foot of the bed. "Give her that letter—in my Bible—Dan."

"What letter, Father?"

"It's in there."

With trembling hands Daniel opened his father's Bible and leafed through it.

"This?"

"Yes."

"Take it out and read it, Mildred," he whispered. Take it away and read. Not here."

Mildred was speechless. For a full minute she stood holding the letter in her hand. Then slowly she walked out of the house and mounted the horse. She felt faint and dizzy.

Before she got around the bend she tore it open. She couldn't wait.

"Whoa, Doc."

Dear Mildred,

You will be surprised to read this letter, but I must confess something before I die.

Mildred's hands shook. Her heart missed a beat. She held her breath awkwardly.

Agnes passed away three years ago. She was good to Dan in her way, but she was not my ideal of a woman or mother. It was not right the way I left after all you and the folks did for me. Mildred, really, you were always my ideal. I'll tell you once more: you are the one I truly loved. I've never been able to understand why you wouldn't consider me just because I was your brother by adoption. I couldn't help that. I know how it looked to others, but I never have been able to forget you.

Has it been Fate or Providence that brought you here to the hills to teach school? You would have to follow me this way when I was trying to run away and forget you. I told Dan we changed our name to Holliday, but never told him why. He doesn't ever need to know, but he does know I'm very sick and sad.

After I'm gone, know once more I love you, Mildred. After you said, 'No,' I didn't care about anything for awhile.

Together, I think we might have been a blessing to the world. I know you aren't married yet. After I'm gone, won't you take Dan and look after him? Teach him the same things Mother and Father taught me. I want him to make good. I've lost out spiritually, but it's all my own fault.

In love,

LEO

Mildred pressed the paper against her heart and burst into tears. All the happenings from her earliest childhood passed before her in a flash. Leo was seventeen months old when she was born. They had been playmates, chums, pals from the first. They had gone to school together, been baptized the same day. Leo grew to be a promising young man. Then one day he left and never returned. He had never written.

His mother and father were heartbroken, for they only partly understood why he left. Month after month they looked for him to return.

"We'll go back, Doc," Mildred turned her horse around.

He was still lying with his hand on his forehead.

"Leo," she said as she touched his arm gently. "I've come back to—to talk this all over with you. You're not going to die—Leo—look at me. I'm not going to let you die."

"Not—going—to—let me?" he asked huskily.

"You're going to live, Leo. You must for Daniel and—and for me—for I've never been able—to forget you—either, Leo. Let's start all over again—I mean where we left off—and be a blessing to Daniel and each other—and the world. Leo, you must get better so we can go back and see the folks."

Leo Foster raised himself on one elbow. Tears trickled down each pale cheek, he smiled faintly, and a ray of hope shone in his tear-filled eyes.

"You—you mean that, Mildred—and this is not—a dream?"

Then the flood of tears broke loose. He buried his face in the sheet.

"It's not a dream, Leo. I really—well," she hesitated; her voice was unsteady. "I didn't really know you held me as your ideal, Leo, but after you left, I knew you were my ideal."

"Mildred!"

Skin For Skin

By Christmas Carol Kauffman, age 49, Hannibal, Missouri
Originally published March 21, 1952
in the Youth's Christian Companion

Bob Marlow's hand trembled a little as he held out the evening paper to his last customer. Any lady living in such a beautiful house should be very happy but he had never seen her smile once.

"Here's your paper, Ma'am."

"Don't call me Ma'am," came the crisp answer. "I'm nobody's Ma'am. Please remember that. My name is Miss Salome Shasty. Did you get it?" She spoke through the screen door.

Bob's arm dropped limp at his side and he almost let go of the paper.

"Yes—um—Miss. Here's your paper, Miss—"

"Shasty I said. See if you can say it."

"Shasty," repeated Bob. His face and his neck felt hot.

"That's better." A hand came out to take the paper. Two diamonds sparkled in the evening sun. "And after this I do not expect you to roll or fold my paper. I want it delivered the way it comes to you. Understand?"

"Yes, Miss Shasty."

Bob hurried down the cement steps. Except for the last customer he enjoyed his paper route. The beautiful house at the end of Hamilton Drive to which Miss Salome Shasty had recently fallen heir, evidently did not make her happy. She always frowned.

But Bob wasn't going to let Miss Salome Shasty make him unhappy. He was working his paper route to get his father a wheel chair.

Bob found her lying face down just inside her screen door. He called twice, but she did not answer.

Bob ran to the corner grocery store and told Mr. Turner to call the ambulance or police.

Both came.

"Her name is Miss Shasty," Bob told the police.

"And who are you?"

"I'm Bob Marlow."

"And do you know this woman?"

"I've been delivering her papers for three months."

"Know anything else?"

"No, sir. She was just like that when I got here."

A column in the next evening's paper was four and one half inches. Miss Salome Shasty who lives alone had been mysteriously scalded and was found lying inside her screen door by her paper boy Bob Marlow. On the kitchen floor was a large puddle of water and on a chair an empty kettle.

Miss Shasty lay semiconscious for several days. Bob stopped at the hospital every evening and laid the paper on the table by her bed. He didn't want to lose a customer. His father, who was crippled with arthritis in his knees, needed a wheelchair.

The fifth evening she had her eyes open.

"Here's your paper, Miss Shasty." Bob stepped close to her bed. She looked sad and scared and haggard.

"Thanks—but—but I'm too sick to read it."

"I've been bringing it in every evening," ventured Bob. "You were always sleeping until tonight. I thought you wouldn't want me to leave it on your porch."

"Course not."

Bob stepped back. Miss Shasty's face was very pale. He pitied her.

"Aren't you any better?"

She shook her head.

"Not a bit?"

She shook her head.

"But you will—"

She closed her tired eyes.

The doctor appeared in the door.

"Come here, lad."

"Me?"

"Yes."

The doctor ushered Bob into a small room down the hall.

"Do you know anyone who knows Miss Shasty?"

"Why, I—I guess, maybe I know her a little. I've been delivering her papers for three months."

"But I must find someone who will give her skin. Otherwise she'll never make it. Do you know anyone?"

Bob stood thinking. "I'll give some."

"You?"

"I don't know who else would. I must keep her for my customer. My father needs a wheel chair."

"What's your name, son?" The doctor placed a warm hand on the boy's shoulder.

"Bob Marlow."

"How old are you, Bob?"

"About fifteen."

"Run along and deliver your papers and try to help me find someone who will donate skin."

"I said I would, doctor. Miss Shasty seems sad and lonely. I don't think she has many friends."

Skillfully the doctor grafted Bob Marlow's skin onto Miss Salome Shasty's back.

Several days later Miss Shasty asked the nurse, "Where's my paper boy?"

"Bob Marlow?"

"Yes."

He's sick in bed, Miss Shasty."

"My paper boy, sick? How do you know?"

"Well, that's what I heard."

"Too bad."

Ten days passed. The doctor led Bob into Miss Shasty's room.

"Here's a young hero, don't you think, Miss Shasty?

"What do you mean?"

"I want you to know that if it hadn't been for Bob here, you might not be here either."

"What do you mean? Please."

"There was no one else but Bob, Miss Shasty, who offered skin for you."

"You mean—you mean?" Miss Shasty tried to get up on one elbow. Her tired eyes filled with sudden tears. "But Doctor Brown, when I said I'd give ten thousand for skin—I never—I never dreamed you'd take it from a boy—why Doctor Brown, you mean you told Bob about my offer and—"

"No, he knew nothing of the offer. I thought we'd wait and and see if you were going to pull through before we told him."

"Bob Marlow," gasped Miss Shasty. "Come here close to me. I want to whisper something in your ear."

The doctor left the room.

Bob bent low. He felt a thin arm encircle his waist.

"Do they hurt yet?"

"What?"

"Your legs or wherever they took the skin from?"

"Some, sure."

"I'm going to make it fifteen thousand, I am. Don't ever tell a single soul, but my colored cleaning woman poured the boiling water on me."

"What?"

"I—I called her a name. I was going to make it hot for her. I was going to give her 'skin for skin,' you know, 'eye for eye,' you know—but—I—I don't think I will now. You wonder why, don't you?"

"Yes."

"It's because of you, Bob. I—I just don't feel like doing it now. She got after me for not being nicer to you and I got angry."

Bob Marlow stood in dumb wonder.

"I'm going to have your picture put on the front page of the paper, Bob. You gave skin for skin, Bob. I never would have dreamed of you doing this for me. You will get your reward. I promise that.

"Then I can get my father," Bob smiled, "the best wheel chair they make, Miss Shasta."

And she, smilingly pressed his arm.

The Littlest Marker

by Christmas Carol Kauffman, age 48, Hannibal Missouri
Originally published November 11, 1951
in the Youth's Christian Companion

This thing of being the smallest might have given me an inferiority complex except for the miracle. To be honest, I was rather discouraged until it happened. You see, I was scarcely ever noticed because I was the smallest marker in the whole cemetery—and way over to the east side, close to the fence. For about two years before it happened, I was nearly covered with tall grass and ragweeds. A pair of gray rabbits even had a nest of little fellows behind me in the tumbleweed pile.

I was put here on Jobie Johnson's grave fifty-two years ago. Jobie's wife, Salorabelle, and her twin boys, Luke and Luther, brought me out here with their horse and wagon and set me up.

I'll never forget the afternoon they came to the monument shop and looked at all the stones. Of course, Mr. Van Zanti could see by Mrs. Johnson's worn shoes and faded calico dress that she wouldn't be able to buy one of the high-priced monuments, so he walked her right past those back to the rear of the store.

He asked her who she wanted the stone for. As soon as Salorabelle said it was to be for her husband, Mr. Van Zanti started talking about Mr. Johnson as though he'd always known him. That was Mr. Van Zanti's method. His sales talk was nothing new to me. I'd been listening to it every day for six years.

I wasn't always the smallest marker. Once I was the very top of an expensive monument. I got cracked when I was being unloaded from a truck. So Mr. Van Zanti cut me off, and fixed up the monument so no one could ever tell the difference. I was chucked away, down under the vase and urn counter in the showroom. That's how I got in on a lot of shoptalk. All I heard in those six years would fill a book.

The second thing Mr. Van Zanti wanted to know was whether or not Jobie left insurance.

"No, sir," answered Salorabelle meekly, twisting and rolling her handkerchief in the palm of her left hand, "Jobie didn't carry life insurance. He left us a four-room house, a garden plot, the horse, the wagon, the furniture, and a few debts, but the boys have done right well by me," she added, beaming on her twins (yet trying not to show pride). "Together we've scratched and saved until we're out of debt."

All the while she kept rolling a wadded-up handkerchief in her hand. "No, sir, Jobie didn't have life insurance, but he had his soul insured against hell fire and all the other everlastin' soul damages, and he left us a good name. The boys can be honest about their papa when they say he lived what he professed—because he did. Jobie wasn't a Sunday Christian and a Monday sinner."

Mr, Van Zanti blew his nose and said with a sort of false warmth that made me chill, "Well, Mrs. Johnson, that's the very kind of folks I like to furnish stones for, for I like to put on the truth. Once it's on, it's there for good."

I wished I cold speak, for I knew good and well Mr. Van Zanti had been working that very morning on Justice T. Dormouth's monument, cutting the inscription his third wife had requested "He was much loved because he loved much." And I knew Mr. Dormouth had been the saloon keeper who died the night after he and his wife had quarreled. I know, because I had heard Mr. Van Zanti read the newspaper to his bookkeeper. Mr. Van Zanti said it looked to him like a case of suicide. He prophesied Mrs. Dormouth would come in and pick out the finest monument in the shop—and that's exactly what she did.

Mr. Van Zanti ushered Mrs. Jobie Johnson and the twins out behind the shop where he kept the "junk," as he called it when customers weren't around. It wasn't five minutes until they were back and Salorabelle was clearing her throat, as though trying to swallow a lump of disappointment, and one of the twins was sniffling.

Mr. Van Zanti was getting bored and wished his customers would leave.

Just then his daughter, Jonetta, drove up in her new Hudson convertible he had given her as a graduation present. She came right in and interrupted without any "pardon me's."

"Dad," she said, "Mother wants you to stop by the florist and get a nice centerpiece and come home right away. We're having important company for dinner Hurry, Dad, so you can get cleaned up and dressed. And be sure to come in the back way."

"I will," he answered shifting from one foot to the other. "Run along, run along."

"Hey there," I felt like shouting. "Don't you know I'm down under here? I've been ignored for six years."

I'll never know why, but Mr. Van Zanti said abruptly, snapping his second finger and thumb, "How much did you say you have, Mrs. Johnson?"

"I have four seventy-five, Mr. Van Zanti," she answered unrolling her wadded-up handkerchief.

Mr. Van Zanti pounced behind the counter and squatting down, dragged me out.

"Here's a little stone, Mrs. Johnson, that I nearly forgot I had. I've been keeping it for someone like you who can't afford a large one. You can have this one for four seventy-five. It will make you a real nice marker."

"It's nice," Salorabelle agreed, "but it's not big enough for many words."

"Not many, Mrs. Johnson, but it's a nice stone."

"But," Salorabelle bent over and placed a warm trembling hand on me (and that was the gentlest touch I'd had in six years), "Isn't it chipped a little here?"

I was beginning to feel excited. I hoped she's say she'd take me. I was anxious to get out of that monument shop.

"Yes," Mr. Van Zanti admitted. "It is chipped a little. That's why I can let you have it at such a reduction. Otherwise it would be eight fifty. It's a fine grade of stone, the finest I carry."

"Shall we, boys?" she asked looking at them confidingly.

"I would," the one answered.

"Papa wouldn't want us to go in debt for one, Mama," the other one said.

"That's so, Luther. We'll decide on it, Mr. Van Zanti, even though it is the smallest. When can we come and get it?"

"I'll place it for you, Mrs. Johnson."

"Oh, no," she objected. "We'll do it ourselves. We'll mix up a little cement, and fix it the way we want it, the boys and I."

Mr. Van Zanti hurried to get his pencil and paper. "J-o-b-i-e, you say?"

"Jobie C. Johnson," Salorabelle said with deep affection. "Born January 5, 1871, died October 22, 1901. And this is what I want you to put below his name: He lived what he professed."

"But—ah—Mrs. Johnson, I cannot put all that on, It would be practically impossible."

"Oh," came her stifled cry, "that is what we had decided on. That was Jobie, he did live exactly what he professed, and so many do not. I wanted it on, Mr. Van Zanti, so the boys would be able to read it there all their lives. Jobie was a good husband and a good father, Mr. Van Zanti. Why Jobie—"

If ever I wished I could have bent myself it was that afternoon, so I could have seen Salorabelle's face.

"Well, let's see, let's see—" Mr. Van Zanti got out his ruler, and gave me a whack. He looked at his watch.

"We'll have to cut it down, Mrs. Johnson," he said, "I mean the letters. That would be," he wrote it down quickly and counted. Twenty-two letters. Impossible. He lived—let's see—he lived his profession. How's that?"

"Well, I guess it means the same thing. Maybe that will be all right."

Mr. Van Zanti measured me again.

"It's still too much, Mrs. Johnson. He lived, that's seven letters. Six more letters is all she'll take. 'He lived' you see will go here."

"I know," broke in one of the twins. "Mama, I know. He lived Christ. Christ has just six letters, doesn't it?"

"It does, doesn't it? He lived Christ? Well that says the same thing."

"That's it then?" asked Mr. Van Zanti. "He lived Christ?"

"Yes, yes, sir," smiled Salorabelle, eyes shimmering with teary mist, lips trembling. "Can we come and get it tomorrow evening?"

"Better make it Saturday," and Mr. Van Zanti followed the three to the door and bolted it without even saying thanks.

I thought Saturday would never come. Mr. Van Zanti moaned and groaned over me before I was finished and declared Mrs. Johnson got a bargain.

"He lived Christ?" asked the bookkeeper. "Of all the strange inscriptions this is the strangest. Does it make sense, Mr. Van Zanti?"

"I guess it does to Mrs. Johnson—and that's all I care."

I couldn't understand it either at the time, but I've learned a lot since I was brought out here to this cemetery. I learned a lot from listening to Salorabelle and her boys. They came out twice a week and put flowers on Jobie's grave, usually wild flowers they had gathered along the way. Salorabelle talked to her boys every time they came out. It wasn't exactly preachy—just common-sense mother talk.

Salorabelle went to Kentucky about ten years ago to visit her sister and while there she took sick and never came back. I doubt if there's anyone buried here who was loved by his wife and children more than Jobie Johnson. Two years ago the twins stopped coming. No one paid any notice to me. The grass soon had me covered up.

Then one evening I heard shouting and laughing in the distance. All at once something hard landed in the weeds in front of me. The rabbits ran in every direction.

I never knew what had happened until the next morning about daybreak. I heard voices close by—across the road, then just outside the iron fence. Back and forth they seemed to be going along the little ditch.

"Let's go inside," one said.

"In the cemetery, Nellie?"

"Why not?"

"But I—I just don't like going into cemeteries even in the daytime."

"Come on. Maybe it went across the fence. We've almost combed the weeds along here. I know it went over there somewhere."

"You go in and look, Nellie. I'll wait here. But it's not in there I'm almost certain."

The next thing I knew two feet were coming toward me. The rabbits crouched close together against my back. Then two hands started rummaging in the tall grass. The rabbits, mother, father, and five little fellows, dashed like they'd been shot at.

"Oh! Freda! Come quick. There's a rabbit nest in here."

"I saw you jump. I—I don't know if I want to come over or not. Such things scare me."

"Freda. Don't be silly. Rabbits are afraid of us. Didn't you see them run? Poor things. I scared them. Why, Freda! I found it. Look, here it is! And come here, Freda. I found something else."

"What, Nellie? A rabbit?"

"Look. Come over. It's a little old tombstone all covered up."

"Well, what of it? You've found the ball, and you'll be getting the reward. Let's go back. Let the tombstone alone."

Two hands were busy pulling weeds and grass away from my face, and I could hear the girl chuckling softly and breathing excitedly.

"This is really something, Freda."

"What do you mean?"

"Why I've got an idea."

"Idea for what?"

"For my unusual experience."

"Well, Nellie Withermill! What's so unusual about finding a little old tombstone?"

"But look. It's a cute little marker, and it's way over here by itself where no one ever notices it. Jobie C. Johnson. Wonder who he was? He lived Christ. Oh, Freda. I've got it."

"Got what? Are you going silly for sure, Nellie?"

"I hope not, but this is going to be my unusual experience."

"Well, what is it? I confess I can't see what you're driving at."

"You can't. Well listen, Freda. Were you at our last M.Y.F. meeting?"

"No, but I heard about it."

"Aren't you going to enter the contest?"

"You mean that essay contest?"

"Yes."

"Of course not. I'm no writer. Are you?"

"I'm going to try. The awards will be trips to three of our city missions, all expenses paid. I'm going to write a story about this little tombstone that's been all covered over with weeds until the rabbits built a nest beside it, then our ball landed over here, and—"

"Yes, and what else? Where's there a story about a little old gravestone? Nellie Withermill?"

"Can't you see it, Freda? There's a story behind this Jobie C. Johnson. Why, there's got to be. It says 'He lived Christ.' I'm going to try to find out who he was, and if he really did live Christ. Maybe Jobie's children have gone to the foreign field as missionaries. Maybe—oh, Freda—maybe a whole list of things."

"Nellie, you're the limit. Come let's go home."

When Nellie came back alone with her paper and pencil, I would have given anything to have been able to talk to her. I could have told her a lot about Jobie's wife and twin boys. And I could have told her a bit about things that I saw and heard out here in forty-eight years. I could have given her enough to write a book.

I never have found out what Nellie Withermill wrote about Jobie C. Johnson and me, but I know she won one of the awards, because she went to visit one of those city missions. I missed her that week, too.

That was two years ago. Nellie still comes and cleans the grass away from me and bring flowers for the grave I mark. Soon after that eventful morning dozens of young folks from Nellie's M.Y.F. came out here to see me. I even had my picture taken, and I think it was put in some kind of a paper with Nellie's story. I gathered that from things I heard.

The very next week after I was uncovered who was brought in here but my old owner, Mr. Van Zanti. His family placed a large expensive monument on his grave.

But his monument has no inscription other than his name and the dates. Perhaps Mr. Van Zanti requested they put nothing else on it. He was smart if he did, for people say what they think of folks, regardless.

Yesterday a young couple came to see me.

"This must be it, Miriam," the young man said. "Jobie C. Johnson. That was grandfather's name. Dad was afraid we might not be able to find it. But this is it. 'He lived Christ.' Dad's often told me the story of this stone."

"Won't you tell it to me, Birney?"

"I will, Miriam. Won't it thrill Dad when we write him and tell him we stopped here to see it?"

Then he took my picture.

If I could talk I'd like to thank Nellie for clearing off the grave I mark. Otherwise I doubt if Jobie's grandson would have found me. I'm the smallest marker, but I'm marking the resting place of a man who lived Christ."

Sometime

By Christmas Carol Kauffman, age 36, Hannibal, Missouri
Originally published March 6, 13 and 20, 1938
in the Youth's Christian Companion

They met face to face at the gate.

"Goin away, Jerry?" asked the old man tenderly and softly as he opened the latch.

The boy made no answer but pushed the gate open rudely with one knee, so that the gate hit the man on the arm. It did not harm his arm for he had on a heavy overcoat. No, it did not hurt his arm but he had a heart even though Jerry had often accused him of not having any. The aged man watched the boy saunter haughtily down the street, his legs making triumphant headway toward town. He began to whistle stray tunes of a new song. With a deep sigh the old man gathered up something heavy.

"Wait a minute Father," called a voice from the door.

"Don't you carry that in by yourself."

She hurried to the gate, wiping her hands on the corner of her gingham apron.

"What is it Father?" She asked with a smile on her pale thin face.

"Oh, some turnips and sweet potatoes and a head of cabbage Miss Daisy gave me."

Together they carried the sack to the house like a pair of tickled children.

"That sure is nice of her." Added the woman thankfully.

"That's Miss Daisy for you." Chuckled the old man, in an old mans way; for he really was eighty and quite feeble, too.

"Here Father," The woman took her father by the arm and led him toward the stove.

"Sit down here. Are you cold?"

"Not really, but it's getting colder right along. It's going to snow before morning."

He rubbed his wrinkled hands.

"Where did Jerry go?"

"He didn't say."

Annie got out a wooden box and dumped the contents of one gunny sack, and her father neither saw her grow suddenly sad, nor heard her moan under her breath. So much had been said, and sighed and cried, that Annie had determined in her own heart to say as little as possible to her father about Jerry's badness and to reprimand him as little as possible in her father's presence. The old man's hair was already snow white, what there was left of it any more, but his heart was whiter yet,

and the only thing that gave him genuine grief was Jerry—
Jerry Charles Campbell.

He was sixteen, tall, dark-eyed, and on the way to being
handsome. He had fine, even teeth and a head of wavy hair that
Jerry combed with pride. His father had died when Jerry was a
tiny boy, too small to remember him. His mother then had to
find employment to keep the older boy in school. Annie, who
was then thirty-five but well and strong, offered to take her
only brother's child and care for little Jerry and love him and
feed him and teach him, and clothe him to the best of her
ability; and why not? Annie Campbell loved her only brother
and loved his baby Jerry too. A sweeter little boy was nowhere
to be found.

Several years later, Jerry's mother married a man from
the South, and she went home with him to lie down and die, it
seemed; or they no more than got a place fixed up until the
word came that she had to leave it. Maybe she wanted to.
That's the way Annie put it anyway. Jerry's brother was
adopted into a wealthy family and was ready for his second
year in high school when an auto crash took him, too.

All this made Father Campbell's hair grow whiter and
whiter, and his step slower and slower. And Mother Campbell
couldn't stay here, either. She took a severe cold, and slipped
away suddenly. That was very hard on Annie and her father,
but they knew she was ready to go and much better off than

they. Jerry cried and cried over her casket until his heart almost broke to pieces. His affection for Grandma was wonderful.

Four years can bring about a great change. Health, wealth, peace, joy, companions that once were realities—where are they now? Like the clouds in the sky, they are they are not. Sin and death change hearts and homes, but Annie and her dear old father did not change. Jerry was the one. Bad boys gradually gained his confidence and sneered at his grandfather's faith. They scoffed at the idea of Jerry's trotting along to Sunday school with "Aunt Annie" and lured him away from the bedtime devotion. They called him "Sissy," and Weak-kneed. And Jelly-fish," until he began to yield. The first time that he missed Sunday school, he felt very, very wicked and could hardly sleep at all that night. The next time he did not come home for dinner to see Annie's tears and hurt look. The first harsh words he flung at Grandpa startled him really; but now they came frequently and with seemingly no degree of a hurt conscience. At the end of four years of Jerry's sinful decline, the Aunt and Grandfather scarcely even expected a kind word from him. He did as he pleased. He came and went at his will which was usually in the early morning, and up late, out and off again—God only knew where. Lazy imprudent and headstrong he was! The devil had led him along by the nose until he had no respect for God's house or for any of God's people. He shamefully abused the old man who had tenderly cared for him and shared every comfort with him these fifteen years, and even mimicked Aunt Annie when she prayed.

"That's all a bunch of bunk!" He said sarcastically one evening, and as he left the house he flung back, "you needn't pray for me, either; you're wasting your breath."

After he had gone, Annie with her arm around her father's shoulder, for she saw how burdened he was, "I'm glad his parent's can't know this; it would kill Emmet."

"We've done the best we know. I never harmed that boy," sobbed the old man pitifully. "He's bad, bad, bad!" He cried. "Jerry Charles is killing me!"

The next day Annie called in a doctor for her father.

"Did he have a shock?" Inquired the doctor of Annie.

"Well—well," she said hesitatingly, "he's grieving over something, I think."

"You must not do that, Grandpa," teased the doctor. "They tell me the penguin dies of grief after its mate is gone."

"It's not my mate, doctor that I'm—I'm grievin' over. It's my boy Jerry. He's—"

"No, no Father, dear," and Annie patted the old man's hand affectionately and kissed it. "Sometime, someday, it may be different."

"Yes, Father, I hope so—sometime."

***

Jerry came in about eleven thirty p.m. dragging his snowy feet over the clean floor and banging the door behind him. Annie had left a cup of cocoa in the pan on the stove, and from her bedroom she could hear him gulp it down, and then go immediately to his own room which was above the kitchen.

It was nine o'clock when he came down for breakfast. Grandpa was sitting in the rocker at his usual place by the east window, humming softly one of his favorite hymns. A sad, sweet peace blessed the old man's face like a benediction, but Jerry interrupted it when he stumbled awkwardly over his feet giving Grandpa a mouthful of evil words on top of it.

"Do you want an egg this morning, Jerry?" Asked Annie kindly.

"Sure," he barked.

"How about working up some wood for me this morning?" Annie proceeded to fry the eggs, two hours past the usual breakfast hour.

Jerry made no answer. He avoided Annie's eyes while he ate in silence. He had a strange cough and seemed uneasy.

"I need wood before I can get dinner," added Annie after a while, "You surely don't expect me to do it." Jerry only sniffed.

"I sure wish you would bring me a pail of fresh water right away" spoke Annie as Jerry left the table.

"Where is the pail?" He growled, and at the same moment picked it up.

He returned with the pail and water and sat it down on the table so hard that some of the water splashed over on the top.

"Where's my gun?" He demanded.

"I don't know, Jerry," answered Annie.

"You do, too. Come on you old—" he caught himself. "You know you hid my gun; an' you tell me where it is, or you'll be sorry."

"Jerry, I tell you the truth," the old man quivered; I have no idea where it is. What would I be doin' with your gun?"

"We'll, it isn't where I put it, so one of you two must have done something with it; and I'll not split or chop one piece of wood until you get it for me; so there!" And he pounded his fist on the table emphatically.

It was all Grandpa Campbell could take. He got to his feet and threw out his hand feebly toward his son's boy. Tears welled up in his eyes and his voice quivered.

"Jerry, he began; "God have mercy on you for your harsh words."

"Mercy nothin', he retorted; "save it for your own self."

"I'm eighty years old and about ready for my grave."

"HUH", came a sneer.

"We always got along. An'—an' were so happy until you started running around with Bill's gang."

Jerry's eyes grew to slits, and his face got red. He inched his way toward the stair door.

"You were always good and obedient," continued the old man; "an we were delighted with you—" His voice broke. "Shared everything we had, an' you were so brilliant in your books, an' promised to be a good Christian man, an'—"

"Christian!" Sneered Jerry.

"Yes; Christian man. Your Sunday-school teacher said there never was one like you, Jerry. Won't you give up the gang before you go too far an' land in the reform school?"

"Ha, ha!" mocked Jerry.

Annie was crying now. All over the room hung pictures of Jerry from baby-hood on up to age twelve. Plump, rosy, and cute! Honest eyes and true and pure! What a difference now!

"You are headed for an awful place, Jerry," continued Grandfather Campbell. "Surely, you do not realize how this is killing me. Your father would turn over in his grave if he knew how you are going." Great tears fell from the old man's eyes.

"Have I ever mistreated you?"

He waited for an answer, but Jerry only hung his head.

"You are going against better knowledge, Jerry. We have taught you the Lord's way since the day your mother died and loved you as our own. I don't want to—to send you away, but unless you choose different we can't keep you." The old man sank into his chair and covered his face with his hands.

Jerry put on his cap and went out of the house with an angry heart. He began to work up some wood in the back yard when a couple of over-grown boys smoking cigarettes came by and whistled, Jerry, whereupon, dropped his ax and stood at the fence talking in an undertone for some time.

"Come on, come on. Let the old Lady split that wood. I let mine do it."

"Yes, but—" Jerry's words failed him. Deep in his soul he still loved Annie to a certain extent, but he was ashamed now to admit it—ashamed of his love for the one who had given her very life for him these fifteen years.

"Well, Jerry," spoke the larger of the two boys, "if you still want to belong to our gang, you'll come along because today's the day. See? If you back out now, we'll squeal on you. Then stand back and see the fuzz fly. Gun loaded?" And he pointed down the street.

Jerry winked an understanding wink. "Got the folks in there belivin' it's—" He shrugged his shoulders. "I'll split just a few more and be comin'."

He took an armful of kindling to the house and was off before Annie had time to get downstairs to thank him. Grandfather was reading his Bible and said. "Thank you, Jerry." That was all.

The boy did not show up for dinner, and both Annie and her father were glad. Miss Daisy dropped in and ate with them. She had such a cheerful way about her, and every time she came, the house rang with hearty laughter once more. They had been friends since away back. Daisy and Annie went to school together, and their fathers took turns coming after them in bad weather.

The dishes were wiped and put away, and Miss Daisy gathered up her belongings to be going, when her face suddenly sobered strangely, and she looked Annie straight in the eyes.

"Where's Jerry?" she asked abruptly. Annie shook her head.

"Where does he hang out when he's away so much?" Annie shook her head again, and old Grandfather Campbell leaned forward.

"Maybe its best we don't know," she suggested. The setting sun made shadows across the room—long purple like. Miss Daisy fumbled with her gloves.

"Well," she said at length, "I don't want to alarm you folks, but I know by accident a few things that boy's into, and unless he gets out of that gang soon, he will land in the wrong place which was never prepared for Jerry Campbell."

"What—what is it?" Annie's breath came fast.

"He's smoking for one thing. I've seen that myself, and I'm afraid he drinks too; and I know he plays cards in those empty boxcars down there; but that's not the worst."

"Oh", shuddered Annie, and her face grew pale; "do tell us." Yet at the same time she felt like stopping her ears so that she could not hear it. How could she bear it? Jerry, who was once so pure and sweet and affectionate and obedient! She motioned for Miss Daisy to come outside to tell the rest. It might make her father have a stroke or something.

"Annie," whispered Miss Daisy, "I hate to tell you because I know it hurts you, but have you been missing anything around here of late?"

"No", answered Annie.

"Or, noticed anything strange around here, I mean strange objects?"

"Well, not that I remember."

"Well, just keep your eyes open, Annie. That gang has sticky fingers. Where do they get the money for their smoke and drink? I must go now."

***

Annie stood on the porch for some minutes and watched Miss Daisy walk off. It was cold out there, but Annie did not notice it. Her face was hot and flushed.

"Annie," her father called softly.

"Yes, Father."

"Put on the lights, it seems so dark."

"Read."

"What shall I read, Father?"

"John, let the supper go, I'm not hungry; I can't get my mind off that boy. What did Miss Daisy have to say?"

"Oh, Father! I'll just read now. Let's cast our burdens over on the Lord. That's what Mother used to do. Don't you remember?"

"Yes."

Annie read from Saint John, portions of comforting Scripture. On and on she read, while her father listened earnestly; heavenly voices, sweet resting places up yonder, everlasting joy and peace undisturbed, brief sorrows here below followed immediately by eternal gladness and happiness —unspeakable. His eyes went shut and his head dropped, and while Annie still read on, her father fell asleep. She touched him gently and would have picked him up bodily and put him to bed, but she knew she could not; she aroused him and told him he better go to bed since he was so tired tonight. He obeyed like a good child. After he was sound asleep, Annie cried privately for a long, long time. A new thought flashed into her mind. Maybe when Father has gone home to be with the Lord; Miss Daisy will come and live with her.

Annie had just fallen into a heavy sleep, when the door opened. It was five minutes past midnight. She sat up in bed and shivered. A strange fear seized her. Since she had gone to bed late, there was still a hot fire in the kitchen stove. Jerry staggered across the room in the dark. He could not find the light. He let out an ugly oath and lunged right into the hot stove, falling with both hands over it. He could not get up. Annie sprang to her feet and hurried to put the lights on. A smothered scream escaped her lips as she snatched the boy off the stove and he fell to the floor with a thud. His face and both hands were badly burned. Annie could smell liquor on his breath. She closed her father's door tightly. Oh, this would hurt him, so she hurried to the phone and called a doctor then, and also Miss Daisy. Miss Daisy said she would come.

Of course the doctor ordered Jerry to the hospital. His moans and screams woke his grandfather, and for a few minutes Miss Daisy and Annie had a hard time keeping him in bed. He dare not see Jerry now. The women told him as best they could, that Jerry accidentally fell on the stove and was burned and the doctor could take care of him, and soon hurried away.

Hours of dreadful suffering followed for Jerry. While on the operating table and during the next few hours, snatches of many secrets were told. He thought he was in jail and was trying to lie out some things but really confessed more than he covered. The wages of sin were painful! Tormented, he found himself in every evil place he had ever been with Bill's gang, and his grandfather's righteous eyes were piercing him through and through. He found himself on the verge of stealing this and that, and just then Annie on the side came on the scene and he denied it. He again found himself on the side streets, but he could not get the cigarette out of his mouth. He was frozen there somehow. He saw his grandfather's face on both sides of the boxcar where the gang met every day, and once his saintly face was on a block of wood he was trying to split. His face and hands burned. Burned! Oh! He was in fire and could not get out! No one came to help him. Prayers! Prayers of bygone days rang in his ears, but no prayers for his suffering body! He thought the doctor was a cop trying to kill him and the boys in the gang were blaming him for the whole thing. On and on he wondered in a maze of utter torment. Then all at once he was in thick, black, black darkness. Lost! Lost! Then—

"Jerry, Jerry", a sweet voice spoke but he could not answer. He could not even open his eyes.

"Jerry, why Jerry." He tried to lift his hand and it felt like pounds of lead.

"It's Annie, Jerry," she stroked his shoulder tenderly. He gave a sigh of relief. His face was covered with a bandage and he was glad she knew it was him.

"What can I do for you Jerry? What can I do for you dear?"

Dear? She had not called him that for a long time. It sounded very comforting. Perhaps she had not seen him in all those hard, bad, evil places.

"Please, stay by me."

"Of course, Jerry. I am here and will stay as long as I can."

"Where is Grandfather?"

"Miss Daisy is with him, but when I go home I will tell him how you are. He is almost too—" she caught herself— "almost too." She thought, maybe he wouldn't even care if Grandfather had a collapse over this?

"What?"

"Jerry, he is so anxious about you."

"Is he?"

"Really, he is."

"Why?"

"Oh, Jerry, he loves you! There could be no other reason could there?"

"I—I don't know." He faltered. "Does he know?"

"Does he know what?"

Oh, she hated to talk about it, but she could see and knew that he had too much to drink. Too much? Oh, if he had not started with that one glass!

"Are you suffering much, Jerry?" She asked with sincerity.

"Oh!" He answered with a moan.

A week passed. Annie and Miss Daisy called and came to see Jerry every day, but not one single friend of Bills even came near. An officer called the hospital one morning full of questions.

"Miss Campbell," said the doctor one morning, "we will have to do some skin grafting on the boy."

"How soon?"

"As soon as we can. Shall I talk it over with him and see if he would be willing to have it taken from his leg.?"

"No! No!" Objected Annie firmly.

Two days later Miss Daisy came into the room.

"How are you Jerry?"

"Oh, not very good, Miss Daisy. When is Annie coming in?"

"Oh, I don't know exactly, Jerry. Sometime soon, I guess."

"Is she sick?"

"Oh, she's not feeling so well; I guess."

"What's the matter?" Jerry was able to see quite plainly now, and he turned anxious eyes on Miss Daisy.

"What's the matter?" He repeated.

"Well, Jerry, your Aunt is up in the operating room right now, giving some of her, of her skin—"

"What?" He tried to sit up, but Miss Daisy stopped him. His body shook, and overwhelming sobs choked him.

"Listen, Jerry." Miss Daisy's voice was soft. "Your grandfather just begged and begged the doctor to take the skin from him, but Annie wouldn't have it."

"OH!"

"He said it was the last thing he could do for you, and he was ready to lay down his life, for—"

"Oh, no!"

"For he was ready to go, and anxious to go—Jerry, for you, and you might realize sometime how, how dearly he loved you, loves you now, but Annie would not hear to it. And so—" She could not finish.

"Grandpa, Oh, Grandpa! When will he be down to see me? Miss Daisy?

Rags

*By Christmas Carol Kauffman, age 42, Hannibal, Missouri
Originally published April 8, 1945
in the Youth's Christian Companion*

Our neighbors have a big old wobbly, shaggy, half-black, half-brown dog that looks a good deal like a dirty oiled floor mop going around on four legs. His name is Rags.

This is not going to be a story about that queer-looking dog, or any other dog, but every time I hear someone calling "Rags" it makes me think of poor little Corley Haskins.

The dreadful thing that I'm going to relate actually happened to Corley a few years ago, and it took place in a town not many miles from here.

Jasper Haskins, little Corley's father, had an occupation that few men earnestly desire. For years he was know throughout the entire county as "Haskins, the Rag Man."

Every day he was perched on the wiggly seat of his ancient wagon, while his half-starved, bony, one-eyed white horse, Doc, wound him about through all the back alleys and off-streets of his home town, or some nearby village. At regular intervals, he would call out in a dry cracking voice, "rags—

paper—scrap iron—rubber—rope, metal of any kind,—rags—
the rags—whoa." Then he'd look this way and that, to see if
some house wife wasn't opening her door to wave him down.
Every evening 'bout dark, Doc pulled Haskins and his day's
gatherings into Riem Brothers and had his collection of junk
weighed on the big scales.

The prices of junk fluctuate from one day to the next,
but Jasper Haskins could usually count on getting at least $1.25
per hundred pounds for rags or rope, more for scrap iron, and
less for paper. In order to make a decent day's wages he had to
bring in a wagon load of goods. He did not always do
this. There were many days that his profit was not over one
dollar, so Effie Haskins, Jasper's wife, took in washing to help
out. There were three little Haskins. Corley aged five, Franklin
D. three, named after the President, and little Minerva Mary
they called Minnie. She was old enough to run fast, and feed
herself, but whenever someone asked Mrs. Haskins how old
Minnie was, she had to stop and count the months.

"Let me see," she'd say, putting the backs of her hands
on her hips. She was a year old the day we et our first ripe
termater, an' that was 'long the middle of July. An' she started
walkin' that day, too. so she's 'round sixteen months now."

One evening a well-dressed woman knocked at the
door.

"I see you have a card in you window 'Washings
Wanted.'"

"Yes-um," smiled Mrs. Haskins, wiping her wet hands on the corner of her apron.

"How much do you charge?" inquired the woman on the porch. She looked in past Mrs. Haskins, and noticed a basket of wet clothes ready to be hung up.

"That depends on the size of the washin'. If you bring me more'n four sheets if will be two dollars an—"

"I see," came the quick answer. "The price really doesn't matter so much, but I'm very particular. Do you put out a nice white wash? I cannot stand dingy-looking clothes. I never had someone who put out first class work for my—"

"Oh," gasped Mrs. Haskins, smiling with it, "you should see some of the washin's I put out. They're as white as the drivvlin' snow."

The woman laughed.

"I'll try you out then. Shall I bring it over tomorrow morning?"

"Yes-um."

"Corley," said Mrs. Haskins, tying on her clothes washing apron, "if that lady brings us her washins' now, maybe I kin get you them new corduroy pants we seen in the winder last week, then you kin go to Sunday school more, maybe."

"Oh, boy," Corley's eyes danced.

The day came when he got those new corduroy pants. Corley ran home from Sunday school squeezing a tiny card in his hand. It was a picture of a little boy standing beside an old man sitting on a bench. An open book rested on one knee, and across the bottom of the card were these four words, "Children, obey your parents." Corley tried to tell his mother everything his teacher had said.

"So you liked it, Corley?"

"Yes, yes!"

"And you say you want to go again?"

"Yes, yes!"

"Corley," called Jasper Haskins one evening driving up to the curb, and bringing Doc to an easy stop. "Come here."

Corley obeyed. He ran over to the wagon and looked up.

"Climb up here on this here ol' wagon with me a while."

Corley obeyed.

Jasper Haskins turned into the first alley and stopped. He opened a gunny sack that had a few potatoes in the bottom of it, and told Corley to step into it.

"Get in that. Corley," he whispered.

"What for?"

"'Cause I said so. Get in."

Corley obeyed

"Now you be real still thar, fer I didn't have no luck taday 'atall."

He gathered up some dirty old rags from a box in the wagon, and put them in the sack around Corley's neck.

"What—what you goin—?" he gasped.

"Be quiet, I said once," and the man stuffed more rags in the sack. You be still now, an' I'll make somethin' terday. No one 'ill ever fin' this out. Now be still."

"Why, Daddy," cried Corley with terror in his voice, "what are you going to do with me?" Tears came to his eyes. He was in rags up to his neck now.

"I said, you be still," came his father's rough answer. "Here's my pocket knife." He opened it, and put it in Corley's little hand. "We'll be down ter Reims in a few minutes. You can help me out this once. I didn't get 'nough terday ter buy a sack a flour. Hush now and stop that cryin'! I'll let the bag untied till we get down thar. How lay over, Corley—I said, Stop that cryin'! It won't take but a minute ter weight these rags, an' I'll dump these sacks off. And when I cough jes' like this, see Corley—" Jasper Haskins coughed— "you take that thar knife an' cut a hole in this sack an' climb out. You jus do that. Now, hush. Don't be a baby. I need the money. Last week I hid a dead cat in a sack of rags, and no one foun' it out, so I guess I can sell a boy once too. If you do this fer me, I'll give you a penny."

"But, Daddy," objected Corley, trying desperately to control himself, "I'll smother! I'll die. I'm getting hot already."

"No, ya won't die. Now lay still. We'll soon be there. Put your head down. I'm going ter tie it shut now."

Corley remembered the verse on his little Sunday school ticket and tried to lie still. But he felt sick. He wanted to scream, but he was afraid to try. It was dark, an darker with his eyes open, than with them shut. His little heart pounded so hard he was sure someone would hear it. His eyes burned and he felt dizzy. He saw queer green lights with his eyes shut so tight. He heard voices. Men talking. The he heard his father laughing, and felt himself being turned over, and other sacks thrown on top of him. Something clicked, and a man said, "O.K. Haskins." The he felt himself being dragged over the cement floor. He listened. After what seemed hours to little Corley, he heard his father cough. Frantically he clawed at the rags with the open pocket knife. The gunny sack was not easy to cut.

Wet with nervous sweat, Corley got up off his trembling knees and looked around. He spied an open door and darted out, and ran and ran until he reached home.

"Mommie, Mommie," sobbed Corley, grabbing her by her dress, with one hand. In the other hand he was gripping an open pocket knife. If I—if I ever—ever—"

"Corley," cried his mother, "what's wrong?" Where have you been? I've been callin' an' callin' for you. What you been doin' with that sharp knife?"

"Oh, Mommie," he choked, "if I ever get a big grown up man an—an have a little—a little boy—I won't never, ever-never tie him up in a sack of rags like that."

"Corley!" screamed his mother in a horrified voice, "What are you tellin' me?"

"Well—he—he—asked me to—"

"To what, Corley?" she shook him a little, she shook the knife out of his hand.

"Daddy—Daddy," he choked, tears streaming down his dirty face. He—he *made* me—get in the sack an—"

"What? You mean—Corley Haskins—you mean in a sack of rags! What for?"

"Why to—to weigh me more," he sobbed "cause he said he needed more money an—"

"Corley!" The mother smote her breast. "You mean your daddy tied you up in a rag sack an' sold you—sold you for rags?"

Corley nodded. "Well—he—he asked me to, Mommie, and when Daddy coughed at me then I cut the sack an' crawled out, an'—an' ran an' ran an' ran home 'cause, Mommie, you know that verse on my ticket, an' Daddy asked me to an—"

"Yes—but Corley, if I 'memember right, there was more to that verse when I went ter Sunday school, an' this weren't in the Lord, or by the Lord, or for the Lord, or whatever it was, cause this was bad an' wicked an'—" She stopped to get her breath. "I'm a-goin; ter have a talk with yer daddy 'bout this awful, awful thing he's made you do. Why—why," she went on breathing fast, "he's the one who oughter go to Sunday school an' learn what's fit an' right, an' what's bad an' wicked ter ask his children ter do." She gathered the trembling child into her arms and held him tight. Tears blinded her eyes.

"I want you ter obey Daddy, Corley, course I do, but listen ter me, honey, if he ever asks you ter do somethin' bad or dishones' again, you come an' ask me first. You poor, little Corley Haskins."

Through the Window

By Christmas Carol Kauffman, age 48, Hannibal Missouri?
Originally published July 6, 13 and 20, 1952
in the Youth's Christian Companion

"Here, Frans," gulped the larger of the two men, "take another drink." With an unsteady paw-like hand he pushed a mug of foaming beer across the hotel room table. Some spilled. He laughed boisterously with no overtone of deception. His bloodshot eyes bulged and the veins at his temples stood out.

"I'd better stop now," hacked Frans, at the same time reaching for his hip pocket. He found it. Wadding his linen handkerchief in his fist he mopped the perspiration that had gathered in tiny puddles in his furrowed forehead. He wiped his messy mouth.

"I'd better stop now, Cletus," he repeated, "but thanks —thanks. You drink it." Frans waved one hand, squinting his bleary eyes. He tried to be dramatic, but he couldn't. He felt as weak as a starved pigeon. He was scared.

"Stop!" snorted Cletus thickly, "why, why—" He scrambled all over the table top for words, then found a few in the yeasty contents of the mug. His blank eyes stared inside the rim, and guiltily, he pulled them out with condemnation.

"You're crazy to stop now, kid," he bellowed, "why our fun's—ha—ha—just begun, Frans, my friend, just begun, an' you—you want to quit?" His laugh bared his crowded crooked teeth. Two were gold crowned. "Here, pal, take it," Cletus insisted, puffing furiously. "There's more downstairs. Here," he got up after several efforts. He lunged across the room, cursing when he knocked over the green upholstered chair.

"Where's that bell? I'll have more sent up. Go ahead—go ahead, Frans. Drink it." More cursings gushed from the man's mouth before he located the bell. He pushed it with all of his two hundred and fifty pounds.

"Cletus," answered Frans, "If I take any more I'll be drunk."

"Drunk? And what of that? Isn't there a bed? Ha. Looks like a good one. Drunk? Scared of getting' drunk, eh? Come on, Frans," and the next minute Frans felt two large hands clutching at the back of his neck. Fingernails dug into his flesh.

"Don't , Cletus. Stop before you hurt me. Let go. Let go. I say I can't drink when you're squeezing me."

A rap at the door.

Cletus opened it.

"You rang, sir?" A young man in uniform bowed slightly.

"I did." Cletus grabbed the door casing. "Bring up three more *True Lager*," he demanded huskily.

"Yes, sir," The bellboy wheeled around abruptly. Cletus fell against the door in closing it.

"Now go ahead, Frans," he said gaining his balance, "drink before I—pour—pour it—down your neck."

"But you see, Cletus," the lad stood facing the older man who towered above him. "You see I better not get drunk today."

"And why?" growled Cletus.

"Because I promised my mother I'd never go that far again. I've already had too much."

"Mother!" hooted the large man with disgust. "Ha—ha —ha—. Mother's baby boy. Say," his hot breath sprayed Frans' face, "you will drink now—that I've—got you—here. You can't—refuse me."

Frans stepped back. His hip struck the sharp corner of the mahogany dresser. His right hand landed on a black leather-bound book.

He started. His breath choked in his throat. "I can't take any more, Cletus," he begged, "and you shan't speak like that about my mother, either. Wait a minute. Don't touch me till— I've said what's on my mind." Frans swayed. Fear and sickness clutched his soul and body. His eyes sought the door. If only he could get out of the room. Why had he allowed himself to accept the invitation of Cletus Van Hoey? Why had he suggested the hotel room? A nice little retreat, he'd called it, where there was privacy, seclusion, safety. Yes, a back room on the fifth floor of the Bridgeford Hotel, a room toward the alley.

Impulsively Frans grabbed his hip pocket. Then pointing a trembling finger under the older man's chin he continued. "My mother was a good woman, I want you to know. She was a Christian, and read her Bible every day. She read it to me when I was a boy and sat on her knee. Don't mock me like that. I"d be better off if I'd followed—her instructions. Before she died I promised her I wouldn't drink any more. Now I've broken my promise."

"Ho—ho," shouted Cletus, blowing his obnoxious breath in Frans' face. "Forget the promise. I had a mother, too, an' she tried that church stuff on me. It's all a bunch of hex. That's all. I promised my old lady—I'd go easy, too—but she'll —ha—ah—never find—out what I done on my runs. She can live her life—an' I'll live mine. I'm in for fun an'—there's no fun without getting' drunk. See?"

"Please don't tempt me, Cletus," pleaded Frans. "You're twice as old as I am. You should know, but you're wrong. This Bible here—"

"Bible?" cut in Cletus indignantly. "Is that what you've got your little hand on? Give it to me."

"Here it is. Are you going to read it?"

"Read it?" came the crusty answer, "This is what I'll do with it." He grabbed the book and twisted it in both hands.

Across the room Cletus Van Hoey plunged in strange peevish fury. With one mad swoop he hit the wall with the Bible. The next instant he swung it above his head yelling hideously; and to the younger man's utter astonishment the Bible fell through the half open window.

Cletus fell. His head struck the knob on the radiator. Blood spurted, and made a nasty blotch on the blue taffeta drapes.

Frans stood in mute alarm. The man on the floor lay gurgling. Then foam came from his open mouth.

Stung with terror and stupidity Frans staggered almost blindly toward the bell.

He rang it again. Would the bellboy never come?

***

The Story Thus Far

Although Frans had a Christian mother, he had his own ideas about how to live. At the beginning of the story he is found in a hotel room with a salesman friend, Cletus. Frans accepts a drink from Cletus but when he refuses more Cletus becomes very angry, backing Frans up against a dresser. Frans' hand falls on a Bible lying on the dresser and Cletus grabs it and throws it though the open window.

***

This second installment of the story begins in an entirely different part of town, with different characters. But the Bible that was thrown through the window enters their lives, too. And in next week's installment that Bible brings together the characters of Part One and Part Two.

Mother Longmire caught Veronica's hand and lifted it to her trembling lips.

I"d rather you didn't go, dear," she whispered softly.

"But why, Mother?" Veronica's deep-set brown eyes looked in her mother's face searchingly.

"I've tried to tell you, Veronica. It's not that I object to you going swimming. But I'd rather that you wouldn't go with Pamela and Netta. They are not the kind of girls for you to go with."

"But I hate to say I can't go now. They're probably on the way." Veronica drew her hand from her mother's clasp.

"Look," she pointed, "they're coming."

"And who is that with them?"

"Oh, it's Raf."

"Raf who, Veronica?" Mother Longmire knit her brows.

"Don't look so troubled, Mother," chided her daughter with a pat on the shoulders.

"But, Veronica," exclaimed her mother with a serious tone in her voice, "you know we don't approve of you going swimming at the Y.W.C.A. with such girls as Netta and Pamela. And he will go along, too, that—Raf you say? Raf who, Veronica?"

"Oh, he's Raf Wickencamp, Mother. He has a crush on Netta. He won't bother me. He's just going to walk along with us."

"But—we don't know this Raf. Where did he come from?"

"Oh, Netta met him in high school. She thinks he's lots of fun. They're here now, Mother. I've got to be going." She pulled herself away.

Mother Longmire followed her daughter to the door, her face sober with concern.

"If you tell them you can't go along, Veronica," she whispered, holding her daughter's arm. "I'll have Daddy take us to the lake tonight."

"Oh, Mother," sighed Veronica, "I'll go this once, and see how it goes. The girls aren't half so bad as you make them."

"But they aren't the kind for you to go swimming with. And now since that young man is going to walk along down with you, I am more certain than before that I do not approve of your going swimming. Oh, Veronica—" and her mother's eyes filled with blinding tears.

"They're calling me, Mother. I must go. Please don't worry over me. I've got to have a little fun."

Veronica went down the steps humming to hide her condemning conscience.

Netta and Raf took the lead. Before they had gone three blocks, Raf took out his cigarettes and offered one to Netta.

Veronica was shocked when Netta took one. She was glad Raf had not offered it while in front of the house.

"You don't need to be so selfish." Pamela called.

"Oh, I beg your pardon," answered Raf, "but I figured you wouldn't want any today. Here?"

"Today?" Pamela took a cigarette.

"Look at the company you're with. Or have you graduated?" Raf winked at Netta with one eye, and kept his gaze on Veronica.

"I have graduated, if that's what you call it."

Veronica was humiliated more when Brother Ames, her minister, passed them at the intersection. He looked at her twice, then tipped his hat.

She felt as though his eyes had pierced her inmost soul. Without a doubt he had seen the cigarettes in the hands of the other three. Perhaps he had seen Raf offering her one. Of course she had not taken any, but he could have imagined she had seen him coming, and had waited until he went by to take one. Oh, horrible thought!

A strange numbness crept into Veronica's legs. She felt a similar one in her stomach.

Netta laughed and giggled as she pranced beside Raf. But Veronica's laugh was as empty as a bird's nest without eggs, and for some reason she was as restless as a little bird who had lost both its mother and nest.

Charlie met Raf at the door of the Y.

"We'll play ping-pong while the girls swim."

"We will?"

After the girls were in the locker room Veronica suddenly exclaimed, "Girls, I forgot my bathing suit!"

"Well, you silly," laughed the girls in unison. "How could you forget that? We supposed you had it in your handbag."

"Well, I'll just watch you then." Veronica wilted.

"A lot of fun that'll be. You can rent one maybe."

"I'd rather not. Since I was so stupid to come off without it, I'll just sit and watch, or go back home."

"Don't go back now."

Veronica was sitting beside an open window, her chin in her right palm. She watched the girls with a dozen others diving and swimming in the huge pool, but her mind did not follow her eyes. It was in the living room at home. All she could see in the pool was the reflection of her mother's tear-filled eyes. She saw not only one pair but a thousand.

Veronica jumped! Her heart raced to her throat. Past her face whizzed something black. It landed with force right into her lap. Her hands went up in dumb wonder. She was too frightened to scream. The color left her cheeks.

It was a book. She held her breath. Then her hands dropped. She opened the book.

A Bible! Why? Where did it come from? Where? She turned in search of the sender. Not a soul was in sight. Behind her was the open window to the alley. But why would anyone be throwing a Bible in the window?

Veronica stood up to look better. She saw no one in the alley. Then a yellow laundry truck passed.

"What was that?" asked several girls from the pool, for they had seen the black object fly through the air. They swam close to the spot where Veronica had been sitting.

"It's a Bible," Veronica answered still stupefied. "All I know is that it landed here in my lap. It's—it's very strange."

"But where did it come from?"

"I don't know. It makes me feel just awful queer. I think it came through that window, but how or why I don't know. It's a mystery."

Mother Longmire lifted her tear-stained face once more. "Dear Lord," she continued, "I know you can still perform miracles. Let something happen to hinder Veronica from going astray. "I've said all I know to say. You do the rest. Please speak to her, dear Lord, today, for Jesus' sake."

***

The Story Thus Far

Frans, a store clerk, is invited to the room of Cletus Van Hoey, a salesman. After several drinks, Cletus, in an angry rage throws out the window a Bible which he has found on the hotel room dresser.

In another part of the city, entirely unrelated to the hotel room scene, Veronica Longmire is disregarding her Mother's wishes as she leaves home to go swimming with two of her rather questionable girl friends. When they get to the YWCA swimming pool she discovers she has forgotten her swimsuit. While Veronica is sitting at the edge of the pool brooding over her disobedience to her Mother, a book suddenly flies through the window. Surprised that it is a Bible, Veronica begins thinking about her Christian life and takes this incident as a reminder that God is following her wherever she goes.

***

As this concluding part begins, Veronica is participating in a jail service led by her pastor, Brother Ames.

Brother Ames nodded. Veronica Longmire stepped forward, facing the row of men behind the bars. On her face was a radiant smile from a new-found joy, and her large brown eyes shone with a beauty that revealed a zeal to tell others

about it. Her hands clasped tightly the Testament she held as
though it was the very life-giving power of her faith and
inspiration. She looked fearlessly into the eyes of the large
scar-faced man directly in front of her. Around his head was a
bandage. He had been sitting in a slouched position on his bunk
pretending to be sleeping. Every now and then from his huge
body escaped a long groan, as though he was tired of life, and
disgusted with every one who lived. He seemed irritated at the
singing of the group.

But the moment Veronica opened her mouth something
awakened his interest. He sat erect. His one hand pushed back
the comic book that lay at his side.

Veronica spoke with a simple eloquence and
unconscious dramatic style. Her earnestness accentuated every
feature of her beautiful face. She seemed to be wrapped around
by the glory of a great ideal.

"I'm so glad I can give a testimony this afternoon for
my Lord," she began. Her cheeks turned a deep pink. Her heart
beat rapidly. "I feel like a transformed person today, for I made
a new consecration to God this morning. It all came about in
such a remarkable way, and Brother Ames asked me to pass it
on to you men this afternoon." Veronica hesitated only a
moment. "I accepted Christ when I was thirteen. At that time I
had a definite experience of salvation, and it lasted until I
started taking my own way. I began to run around with the
wrong bunch. My parents objected, but I failed to take their

advice. I tried to act happy, but I knew deep down in my heart I wasn't. My mother did not scold, but she prayed. There's a power in a Christian mother's prayers.

Yesterday I was sitting by an alley window in the basement of the YWCA watching the girls in the swimming pool. I won't tell what transpired at home before I left, but I felt very wicked as I was sitting there reviewing my recent past. I knew I had been disobedient. The other girls were having a great time, but nobody knows how wretched and miserable I was. I knew I had lost my fellowship with God. It's a terrible feeling. All at once a Bible came flying through the window behind me, and landed in my lap. I was startled."

The man behind the bars stopped breathing. He ground his teeth, then bit his lip.

"Where the Bible came from I do not know. I'll likely never know. The flyleaf was gone. I looked out the window, but no one was in sight. Then a feeling of deep awe came over me. I felt as though the Bible had been sent to me straight from God for a purpose. It made me realize as I never did before that God was following me wherever I went. And I'm so glad today He does. I thank God for this experience, because I went home and did some serious thinking, and some serious praying too.

"This morning in church I reconsecrated my life to God. Perhaps if I had continued to disobey my parents, I might have gone much deeper in sin.

A while ago we sang two songs, 'Welcome for Me' and

'Jesus Reaches Out His Hand and Helps Us Through.' That's my testimony as a young Christian. I'm so glad Jesus reached out His hand and tossed His Word right into my lap, and then helped me through my difficulty. He gave me a welcome to come back to Him and I came. The joy in my heart now is unspeakable, and full of glory. My earnest prayer is that everyone of you men will have some kind of an experience that will bring you to Christ too. It's the only happy life to live."

The man in cell Number 29 folded his arms tightly across his breast. Beads of perspiration stood in rows across his forehead and upper lip. He swayed for a moment as though he was fainting, then, turning abruptly, walked to the farther end of the cell and sat down on the edge of his bunk with his back to the little band of Christians.

"Would you like one of these Gospels of John, Mister?" asked Brother Ames. "It's for you for the taking."

"Nah," came the rough answer, "not today." He did not turn.

"Not today? Then shall we remember you in our prayers?" asked Brother Ames.

"Nah. Spend your time praying for the other guys. Go on. Let me alone." He buried his face in his hands and shrugged his shoulders.

"We'll go down to the end of the corridor and sing two more songs," announced Brother Ames.

The group of young people followed.

In the cell a young man was standing with both hands on the bars, his face pressed hard against the irons.

"Come here, Miss," he called. He looked straight at Veronica.

"Who? Me?" asked Veronica.

"Yes, you."

She stepped closer. His misty blue eyes were red from crying. He looked hurt, disappointed, smitten.

"What can I do for you, sir?" she inquired.

"For one thing you can pray for me."

"We will all do that, sir."

"Thank you. God knows I need it. I—I heard your testimony."

"You did?"

"I was listening. I heard most of it. I know it was you, for I strained every nerve to see. You said a Bible landed on your lap as you sat at the YWCA?"

"Yes, sir."

"The YWCA swimming pool is to the back of the—that is—I mean the windows are to the alley across from the Bridgeford Hotel, aren't they?"

"I believe so."

"Then I can tell you where the Bible came from."

Veronica took half a step back. She lifted her head in surprise.

"You—you can?"

"Someone threw it out the fifth-story window of the hotel."

"Threw it out the window? But why?"

"He was angry with me, and drunk besides. It was evidently a Bible someone had left there."

"I never thought of it coming from the hotel. If it had been a Gideon Bible I might have thought of that. But why did the man throw it out the window?"

"I was in that room with Mister Cletus Van Hoey, a salesman. I work in the Haught Shoe Store. Cletus often comes in. Yesterday he persuaded me to go with him to the hotel, saying he wanted to talk over some business matters. To make my story short—well—he offered me a drink. I took it. I took more than one." The young man's voice broke. Tears trickled down both cheeks. He wiped them away quickly.

"I had a good mother, Miss. She taught me right if ever a mother did. But I had ideas of my own, too. I heard what you said. I went a lot further than you did, I'm sure. I was plenty bad. It all started from running with the wrong gang. My mother often pleaded with me, but I went ahead and broke her heart."

The young man covered his face with his handkerchief. He shook with sobs.

"If she were living and knew I was in here, she'd be dead before night. I promised her before she died I'd quit drinking and go straight. Yesterday I broke my promise, and she's been gone only a month. That Cletus Van Hoey aimed to rob me, I think, but he didn't get that accomplished."

"He's in here somewhere too. At least he should be. He got pretty rough with me up there in the hotel room when I refused to keep on drinking with him, and I guess the bellboy reported us. Cletus fell and cut his head on the radiator. The cops came. I did not hit him, although he tried to make out I did. But I'm in here now, and this is what I get for breaking my promise. I'm ashamed of it. I have a nice girl friend, but I'm afraid she'll turn me down now. I'm so—oh, so ashamed. The Bible was on the dresser as I told you, and it made me think of my mother. If I remember right, Cletus was mad because I mentioned my mother and something about the Bible—it's not all exactly clear to me, but I do remember him throwing it out the window in a rage."

"Oh, and so that's where it came from, and not from God?"

"I wouldn't say that, Miss. Cletus Van Hoey threw it— but—I guess God saw to it that it landed on your lap—instead of in the sewer hole."

"That's so. Oh, isn't it just like a story, Brother Ames? Did you hear it all?"

"I've been listening, Veronica. God's Word will not be destroyed. It shall accomplish wonders, and it certainly does. Mister—friend—won't you accept Christ today, and let Him be the Master of your life, too? He'll help you over these difficulties if you only give him a chance."

"I have already decided there must be a change. I do want to live right if I ever get out of this mess."

"You don't need to wait until you get out of here, my friend. Take Jesus right now, just as you are. He will save you in less time than it took that Bible to go from that hotel window through the window below. Won't you say yes, Mister—?"

"Just call me Frans."

"Frans, then don't put it off. The invitation is 'Come.' Come right now."

"I—will!" He cried, and the peace of God lit up his face like a heavenly benediction.

"When I get home," Veronica whispered, as they walked down the steps of the jail, "I am going to write a story about this experience for our youth magazine. I will call it 'Through the Window.' Oh, I never was so happy as I am right now. But that poor man who did the throwing. How can we win him to Christ? He was very sour."

"I know, Veronica," said one of the girls in the party; "you write the story and give him a copy of it."

"That's exactly what I'll do. I'm going to find out who he is, and where he lives, and let him know that the Bible he threw through the window was not destroyed but led two people back to Christ."